"Lady, Your Whole Life Is A Lie."

Kane felt Brenna's slim fingers curl into a fist beneath his own.

"Would you care to explain that?" Brenna challenged.

"Where do you want to start?" he drawled. "With eyes that show you're hungry for my touch? With lips that moved over mine, making the damnedest sounds of pleasure I've ever heard? With a body that shivered with delight when I touched it? Or with a briefcase, suit and neat little pumps, the uniform of the lady executive?"

Brenna jerked her hand out of his grasp. "I own a business. I dress professionally."

"Of course, but are you one-dimensional? Have you buried your feelings so deep that you don't even admit they exist, just so it's easier to control things?"

Brenna looked away. Was it too much to be allowed to plan her own life? She tried to ignore the sense of loss creeping over her as she contemplated the future without Kane.

Dear Reader:

I hope you've been enjoying 1989, our "Year of the Man" at Silhouette Desire. Every one of the twelve authors who are contributing a *Man of the Month* has created a very special someone for your reading pleasure. Each man is unique, and each author's style and characterization give you a different insight into her man's story.

From January to December, 1989 will be a twelve-month extravaganza spotlighting one book each month with special cover treatment as a tribute to the Silhouette Desire hero—our *Man of the Month*!

Created by your favorite authors, these men are utterly irresistible. Love, betrayal, greed and revenge are all part of Lucy Gordon's dramatic *Vengeance Is Mine*, featuring Luke Harmon as Mr. May, and I think you'll find Annette Broadrick's Quinn McNamara...*Irresistible*! Coming in June.

Don't let these men get away!

Yours,

Isabel Swift
Senior Editor & Editorial Coordinator

RITA RAINVILLE
A Touch of Class

Published by Silhouette Books New York
America's Publisher of Contemporary Romance

SILHOUETTE BOOKS
300 East 42nd St., New York, N.Y. 10017

ISBN: 0-373-05495-5

First Silhouette Books printing May 1989

RITA RAINVILLE

has been a favorite with romance readers since the publication of her first book *Challenge the Devil*, in 1984. More recently, she won the Romance Writers of America Golden Medallion Award for *It Takes a Thief*. She was also a part of the Silhouette Romance Homecoming Celebration, as one of the authors featured in the "Month of Continuing Stars."

Rita has always been in love with books, especially romances. In fact, because reading has always been such an important part of her life, she has become a literacy volunteer and now teaches reading to those who have yet to discover the pleasure of a good book.

Southern California is home to this prolific and happily married author, who plans to continue writing romances for a long time to come.

For Don—
again
and always

One

No one had ever said that life was fair.

Or easy.

That thought jolted Brenna MacKay as she closed the office door behind her, stopping at the sight of the big, dark-haired man leaning against her desk, arms folded across his broad chest. Hard gray eyes made a quick head-to-toe pass over her then stopped, studying her face. His silence sizzled like a burning stick of dynamite in the quiet room. To someone already burdened with a guilty conscience, it spoke of predators and traps about to be sprung.

No, she thought again with another quick glance at his hard face, life wasn't easy. So why had she ever thought it would be a simple matter to say goodbye to Kane Matthews?

Not that she'd actually *said* it, she amended silently, her greenish gaze drifting down to the crumpled letter he held in his hand. Wincing at the mangled condition of the note, she silently acknowledged that her method of delivery wouldn't win any medals for valor. True, she had had her doubts at the time; however, not being a complete fool, she'd opted for expedience—knowing that she'd be long gone when he read the message.

It hadn't been an easy decision. Now, looking up into silvery-gray eyes, she wondered again if it had been the right one. Lowering her gaze to the stubborn set of his jaw, she gave the matter a full three seconds of thought.

Yes, it had.

The very fact that he was here in her office, just itching for a fight, convinced her. When she wrote the note, she had been in no condition to argue with him. As far as that went, she still wasn't.

"Hi," she managed brightly. "Just happen to be in the neighborhood?" Her voice was too breathless, the words a bit too flippant, she decided with a wince. It didn't matter, she realized a moment later. His mind was on other things.

"What do you mean you aren't going to see me again?"

Brenna stiffened at the sound of his soft, deep voice. It was too soft, she decided, a knot in her stomach reminding her just how much she hated confrontations.

Sidestepping him with the precision of a tightrope walker, she dropped into her chair, casting a quick, yearning glance at the empty coffeepot. With an effort, she kept her voice low, soothing. "That's not exactly what I said."

Kane straightened, looming over her, ignoring her quiet statement.

Forcing herself to sit still, Brenna returned his steady gaze. It wasn't easy. Kane wasn't a predictable man—far from it—and she had never claimed to be psychic, but she knew that in the next few seconds he was going to utter the last words in the world that she wanted to hear. Closing her eyes in resignation, she waited.

It didn't take long.

"We're lovers, Brenna. You don't end something like that with a polite letter of dismissal."

Shaking her head slowly, she took a deep, calming breath. "Not lovers, Kane," she said definitely. "We slept together. Once. Last night."

Pleased and a bit surprised by the steadiness of her voice, she added, "And since it's ending as suddenly as it began, I don't think we could actually be called—"

"Lovers." His voice was as flat and stubborn as the expression in his smoky eyes. "A few hours ago I held you in my arms and pleasured every sweet inch of your body." Kane's eyes narrowed in pure male satisfaction at the sudden wash of color in her cheeks. "And before the night was over," he reminded her in that soft, maddening voice, "you did the same to me."

Brenna's expression would have stopped a lesser man in his tracks. It had no effect on Kane Matthews. None. Whatsoever.

Reaching out a large hand and touching her cheek in a whisper-soft caress, he said, "You flowed over me like wild honey, and you wanted me every bit as much as I wanted you. Now you're trying to pretend it never happened. It won't work, Brenna. Amnesia's usually the result of shock, not passion."

Defiantly she laced her fingers and settled her hands in her lap. She wouldn't lose her temper, she told herself. Successful media and etiquette consultants were above such displays. Besides, she wouldn't give him the satisfaction of knowing that he'd rattled her. She would stay calm and serene if it killed her. Tilting her head in a gesture of polite interest, she waited for him to continue. When he didn't, she slid a cool, oblique glance up at him, the corners of her mouth lifting in satisfaction. He looked as though he wanted to snatch her up and sear right through her control—the control that, unfortunately, she'd lost so thoroughly the night before.

Instead, when he finally spoke, his words were offhand, as if they'd spent a thousand nights together rather than one. "I thought you were in the shower when I got up. I was going to join you when I found this on the dresser." He opened his hand to show her the crumpled paper. The way his long fingers had methodically mashed it into a small wad wiped away the last remnants of her polite expression.

"Brenna," he commanded softly, reaching down again and tilting her chin until her reluctant gaze met his, "tell me why you're running. What we had last night wasn't a casual, one-night stand and you know it."

"I explained that," she began cautiously, noting automatically that even though he was in a raging temper, he had it under control. Just barely. Then she thought of something she should have realized when she first met him—or at least when she scribbled the note: Kane's success in business proved that he was a stubborn, aggressive opponent who fought for what he wanted. And apparently, at this particular moment, what he wanted was *her*. He definitely wasn't the type to read a jumbled, rather desperate explanation, and then wait meekly for a telephone call. As far as that went, he probably wasn't meek about anything.

"I told you—"

"That you needed time to think," he interrupted coolly, dropping the wadded note precisely in the center of her oak desk. "Okay. You've got it."

Brenna blinked in wary surprise. "I do?"

His dark lashes lowered, concealing the expression in his eyes before he added, "Within reason. I won't rush you back into bed, but I'm not about to let you scribble a few lines on a piece of paper and walk out of my life."

Bracing her hands on her desk, Brenna fought a rush of fury. It was as sudden as it was unexpected. "Thank you so much," she said icily, shooting him a lethal glance. In the next instant she tossed control to the wind, demanding, "What do you *mean*, you won't rush me back to bed? I've got something to say about it, you know. A lot to say, as a matter of fact. Just who the devil do you think you are?"

Eyes gleaming at her flash of temper, he murmured provokingly, "I thought we'd already settled that. Your lover."

Brenna surged to her feet and paced to the other end of the small room in seething silence. Of all the maddening, pigheaded men! She must have been out of her mind. Utterly insane. How could she—even for one solitary minute—have thought he was the right man for her? Where on earth was the restrained, cool person she'd been so drawn to? What had happened to the man who had made no secret of his attraction to her, but had lazily, firmly, kept his emotions in check? Was he a complete figment of her imagination?

Swinging around to the small coffee maker, she jabbed a button and watched the red light go on, mulling over his flat statement. Lovers? No way. She might not have shown much of a knack for self-preservation last night, but this was another day and she was just a tad wiser.

When coffee began streaming into the pot, she turned back to face him and said determinedly, "We've settled nothing. Spending one night together doesn't mean that…'' She hesitated just long enough for him to pick up the slack.

"Doesn't mean what?"

"Whatever you seem to think it means!" she finished raggedly.

He stared at her for a moment, then nodded toward the crumpled note. "You said you'd made a mistake and you needed time. I'm here to tell you, lady, that the only mistake you made was not recognizing what we found last night." He glanced down at his watch, then back at the taut line of her shoulders as she stared in apparent fascination at the diminishing stream of coffee. "But we'll have more time to talk about it over dinner tonight."

Brenna stiffened. *Dinner?* Did he think she was crazy? Just a few hours before it had taken every bit of courage she'd had to ease out from under his arm, leaving him sprawled over three-quarters of the large bed, his naked body conveying a ridiculous degree of contentment, while she threw on her clothes, scratched out a hurried note and crept silently from his house. And he wanted to take her to dinner? Fat chance! She hadn't had time in which to make any definite plans, but her immediate policy called for keeping as far away from him as possible.

"I don't think that's a good idea, Kane." She turned back to him, determined to end it here and now.

"No dinner?"

She shook her head.

A chill worked its way down her spine at his level look. It told her that she wasn't going to like his answer.

It was right, she didn't.

"Then I guess we'll have to do it the hard way." He extended a long arm and snagged the only other chair in the room. Placing it at right angles to her empty one, he shrugged out of his jacket, folded it neatly and put it on top of her filing cabinet before he sat down. Stretching out his legs, he contemplated the tips of his gleaming cordovan shoes, ignoring her anxious stare.

When the coffee maker gurgled to a stop, Brenna turned her back to him, pathetically grateful for the momentary reprieve.

"I like mine black."

"I know," she muttered, annoyed by the bland assurance in his voice.

"Filled to the top."

"I . . . know."

"No sugar."

"I *know*."

Brenna added cream to hers, set his in front of him, and then moved her chair to a safer distance before easing into it.

"It's hot," she warned. Idiot. Of course it was hot.

"I have plenty of time."

Wrapping both hands around the cup, she took a swallow and closed her eyes.

"It won't work," he told her finally. "I'm not going to disappear."

Her lashes lifted. Pointing to his mug, she said hopefully, "You're coffee's gone."

"There's plenty more, isn't there?"

"Yes." Unfortunately. "I thought you said you had a meeting scheduled this morning."

His shoulders lifted in a massive shrug. "It'll wait."

"Kane, you can't stay here forever!"

"I don't intend to. Only as long as it takes."

Staring at his expressionless face she thought of the words she drummed into her clients. Stay calm. The world may fall in around your ears, but don't panic. The one who remains calm stays in control and is the eventual winner. Control was always the key in a tight situation.

But it was hard to be composed when a hundred and ninety pounds of pure male stubbornness stared back at her. It was undoubtedly one of the qualities that had contributed to Kane's reputation as an aggressive businessman—it also had a great deal to do with his success in the competitive computer software field. Her eyes skimmed over a chin that was just as unyielding as the rest of him, wondering how on earth she'd managed to overlook such an obvious characteristic. Obstinacy wasn't a trait that she found endearing. She should have expected it, though.

Kane wasn't a man who smiled a lot, however, Brenna acknowledged to herself ruefully, that was one of the things about him that had initially intrigued her. Her first sight of him at the Santa Barbara business conference should have warned her, she thought with belated insight. She'd had the fanciful impression that she was watching a Doberman pinscher stroll through a pack of tail-wagging spaniels. Too bad she hadn't remembered that even well-trained Dobermans were as dangerous as they were disciplined.

Of course, it was his very lack of aggression that had lulled her into a false sense of security. But if she had taken a closer look at him first, she might have saved herself a lot of grief, she reflected. Everything about him shouted that he was a man who gave orders and expected them to be obeyed without question. Even his hair, as dark brown as the coffee he was drinking, was extremely well disciplined. It never strayed forward over his brow, never looked rumpled. Straight, heavy brows, equally dark, framed eyes that could intimidate without even trying. His chin was out-and-out stubborn. Add that to six feet of muscle and what do you have? she asked herself disgust-edly. Seventy-two inches of trouble!

He was definitely the man in charge—of himself and everyone foolish enough to get in his way. Which, of course, was the whole problem. Years earlier, she had vowed to be in control of her own life and she wasn't about to turn over the reins to anyone. Ever.

"Damn it, Kane," she burst out in agitation, "you may be able to make people wait, but I can't. I have several important appointments this morning and I don't have time to play games."

"I'm not playing."

Brenna's voice rose a notch at his flat response. "What on earth do you *want*?"

"You." A wry movement lifted the corners of his mouth at the instinctive shake of her head. "Tonight. At dinner. To talk."

In an effort to avoid his gaze, Brenna glanced down at his strong, well-shaped fingers with their fine sprinkling of dark hair. Involuntarily she thought of the night before—his hands on her, touching, stroking, crumbling her de-fenses. Just as quickly, she cast the memories aside. It was too soon, far too soon, and he was much too close.

"Okay," she decided abruptly, moving away from the desk. A meal was a small price to pay. Anything was bet-ter than the refined torture of having him sitting there, waiting implacably, making silent demands that she couldn't—wouldn't—satisfy.

"I'll be ready at six-thirty, but we eat at a restaurant, not at your place." Last night had taught her *something*. "If it's so all-fired important, we'll talk, but I have to be home early. I have a lot of work to do."

She watched Kane get to his feet with a decisive air and silently shrug into his jacket, forcing herself to remain still when he moved toward her. He stopped in front of her, lifting his hands to frame her face. In spite of herself, she stiffened. His eyes lingered on her mouth until she swallowed dryly, then he brushed his thumb across her full, lower lip in a shockingly sensual caress.

"Six-thirty," he agreed evenly, and walked out, closing the door without a sound.

For a second Brenna went limp with reaction, slumping against the small oak counter as she took a quick inventory of her body. Her stomach informed her that the scene had been every bit as nerve-racking as she'd expected. Her knees, which were fighting to keep her erect, agreed. The rest of her seemed surprised that she'd survived the ordeal intact. Of course, a part of her brain reminded her, she had only been granted a reprieve; there was still tonight to get through.

"Damn!" Brenna softly exhaled the word. With a slightly shaking hand, she poured another cup of coffee, then retreated to her chair. Closing her eyes, she rested her head against the high back of the chair, frowning at her dismal parade of thoughts.

It wasn't going to be easy. If Kane had his way, it wouldn't even be possible. Saying goodbye was no longer somewhere in the category of a simple skirmish; it was lining up right there along with World War III!

When the doorknob rattled, she didn't so much as lift an eyelash. It wasn't Kane; he had what he wanted—for now. She was safe, at least until six-thirty.

"Hi, did I just see Kane leaving?"

Brenna opened her eyes and looked at the speculative expression on the face of her best friend and partner, Julie Fontaine. Only her head was visible through the narrow opening of the door.

"Um hmm."

"What was he doing around here so early?"

"Oh...we had something to discuss," Brenna said vaguely, avoiding Julie's curious gaze.

"Such as when you're going to put him out of his misery?"

Brenna blinked. Ah, what the hell, she reflected. After the way the day had begun, it couldn't get any worse. She might as well let Julie have her say. Deciding to give bland surprise her best shot, she raised her brows and murmured, "He doesn't look like he's suffering."

Julie swung open the door and breezed in, dropping down into the other chair. She tackled the conversation the way she did a business problem: head on. "Come on, Brenna, you know what I'm talking about. For six weeks Kane Matthews has been treating you like a piece of porcelain—no mean trick for a man who looks like he ordinarily walks in and snatches what he wants. I can't help wondering when he's going to pounce."

Even as she silently acknowledged her friend's perceptiveness—and wished she'd had a fraction of it during the last six weeks—Brenna hedged. She might have made a gigantic mistake, but that didn't mean she was ready to admit it! "I know he has the reputation of being a maverick, but I've never seen that side of him." Until last night.

"Well, you can bet your sweet patooty that he's done something to earn it."

Something? Brenna shifted restlessly in her chair. He'd probably done plenty. And her life would be a lot less complicated right now if she had just figured that out sooner, she reflected gloomily.

Julie swung around and looked behind her. "Ah, coffee. Want some more?" Quickly she filled two cups and sat back down. "Now," she ordered. "What's going on? Why was he here so early?"

"What was your first impression of Kane?" Brenna asked with genuine curiosity, hoping at the same time to sidetrack her friend.

"That you had a tiger by the tail," Julie said promptly.

Brenna shot her a wry look. "You might have told me."

"You mean you actually bought that quiet, restrained act, the 'I'll look but not touch' scenario?"

"It wasn't so hard. I thought he was dazzled by my brilliant mind."

Julie looked at her in disbelief, running a slim hand through tightly curled chestnut hair.

"Your stunned expression isn't very flattering," Brenna informed her dryly. "I thought maybe, just this once, I'd found a man who was interested in something besides body measurements."

"And I think you thought right."

"Then what—?"

Julie held up her hand, palm out, stopping the words. "The fact that he appreciates your, uh, inner qualities doesn't necessarily blind him to the rest of you, you know. For the last six weeks, you've seen each other almost every evening and weekend, so it couldn't have just been lust on his part. If it had been, we wouldn't be having this discussion."

"Damn it, it's been nice this way," Brenna said, dropping her cup on the desk with a small thump. "We were *comfortable*."

"Maybe you were, but I don't think Kane would describe his condition as . . . what do you mean *were*?" Julie pounced on the word with the speed of a hungry cat downing a fat mouse.

"Nothing." Brenna backtracked hastily. "I just mean that I don't see why things have to change. Why are you looking at me like that?"

"My friend, where were you when all the other little girls were busy learning about that old devil, sex?"

"Not everyone has your consuming interest in the subject," Brenna informed her grumpily, opening her appointment book and staring down at the page as if it contained the answer to her latest problems—all six feet of it.

"But most people learn eventually," Julie persisted, ignoring Brenna's don't-you-have-something-to-do? expression with the ease of familiarity, concentrating on the more important issue. "I admit, some are slower than others, but this is a case of arrested development if I ever saw one. Didn't you listen to a single thing I said while we were in college?"

Brenna looked up with an exasperated sigh. This was definitely not what she needed right now. "Julie, we roomed together for four years and you never stopped talking. You surely didn't expect me to listen *all* the time?"

"Did you pay attention to anything?"

"Yes."

"What?"

"You told me to put spray starch on my tennis shoes to keep them white, and I did."

"And? Did it work?"

"No. When I washed them they got sticky."

With a flick of her hand, as if swatting a fly, Julie said, "You probably didn't shake the can hard enough. Anyway, that's not what I'm talking about and you know it. I'm personally involved here—my reputation is on the line. You were my roommate for all those years and you still believe that Kane Matthews is only interested in your *mind*?''

"Not anymore! I—''

Julie waved her down again. "How could you not know that the man's an absolute menace? All you have to do is look at him.''

"Call it a quirk,'' Brenna said with a sigh. "I'm honest with people and I expect them to be the same with me. That first day, he asked me out to dinner to discuss some business and we then spent the evening together. We talked for hours. He didn't even kiss me good-night. Then we just sort of fell into the habit of being together.''

Julie snorted. "Habit? Like dining with an octogenarian uncle?''

Hardly. As time passed, smoky eyes had gleamed with hunger and strong arms had frequently tugged her close to his hard body. But the hunger had been controlled and, gradually, she had been drawn to the fire in him, flirting with the flame.

"Are you listening to me, Brenna?''

"No. Go to work and leave me alone.''

"Not until you tell me how he made mad, passionate love to you last night.''

"*What?*'' The pencil slipped out of Brenna's hand and slid across the desk. Julie reached out and snagged it before it hit the floor. In that split second, Brenna adjusted her expression to what she hoped was one of mild amusement. "What a peculiar thing to say,'' she managed weakly.

"Nothing strange about it at all,'' Julie retorted. "I just figured six weeks would be the outside limit of his patience.''

"That's not saying much for my resistance.'' If she ever told anyone about last night, it would probably be the maddening woman across from her. But not today; it was too soon. Perhaps she'd talk about it after she had worked her way out of the mess she was in, but right now she was no closer to a solution than she'd been when she crept out of Kane's front door.

"Don't get your dander up. I know you're as tough as old boots," Julie drawled, her gaze lingering on the faint shadows beneath her friend's eyes. "But even *your* iron control will be a lost cause when Kane decides to move."

"What do you mean?"

"Well, probably all he needed was one look at you to know that he was going to have to haul out the big guns. The way I see it, it's just a matter of when he decides to pull the trigger."

"For God's sake! You make me sound like the original ice maiden."

Julie grinned. "On the contrary. Men love you. They think you're warm and sexy, they want to take you home to Mama. Then, before they know what's happening, they hit the barrier you set up. And the crazy thing is, you do it so well it takes them a while to realize that instead of a new woman, they have a buddy, a friend." She stopped, stared at Brenna across the width of the desk, then plunged on. "But my crystal ball tells me that Kane isn't going to be as accommodating as the rest of them."

Grateful that her annoying friend didn't know just how true her words were, Brenna cast her a harried glance. "Julie," she said desperately, "Mr. Ennis is going to be calling any minute to check out the seminar I'm doing for him next week. Will you please let me get back to work?"

"Okay, I'm gone."

Why on earth did the fact that she chose to be in charge of her own life bother so many people? Brenna wondered, sliding back in her chair. God only knew it was a right she had earned. And until six weeks ago, her life had been absolutely on target. She had a large circle of friends, her social life was as busy as she wanted it to be, and business was flourishing—so much so that she and Julie had decided to move out of their present office into larger quarters.

What it boiled down to, she told herself resolutely, was that a man like Kane Matthews had no place in her well-ordered life. At least not the Kane she'd discovered last night in bed, not the one she'd confronted a few minutes ago. He was a far cry from the man she thought she'd found, the one who would share her dream of a stable life, a life of harmony and tranquillity.

Tranquil? Kane Matthews? He was as peaceful as a buzz saw! And she wasn't about to have her life turned inside out by someone like him. But leaving a note had been the wrong way to handle the situation, she decided with a frown, struggling to consider the matter from his viewpoint. She should have stayed to discuss the situation. But it wasn't too late. Tonight she would tell him calmly and rationally that it simply wouldn't work. He was a logical man; surely he would listen to reason.

And with that optimistic thought, Brenna looked down at her watch. She had exactly nine hours and forty-three minutes in which to find the right words.

Two

———

"What do you mean, it doesn't make sense? Damn it, if you'd quit shaking your head and listen to me, you'd see that it makes *perfect* sense," Brenna insisted, pointing her fork at Kane. Her voice was slightly higher than her normal husky alto, showing her frustration as clearly as did the glare she was directing across the table.

They were in one of San Diego's oceanfront restaurants, at a table next to a large window where they could watch the creamy waves gliding across the sand, followed by lacy trains of froth. The tables were placed far enough apart to insure privacy, and flickering candles provided an intimate halo of light.

The atmosphere was wasted on Brenna, Kane decided, calmly slicing off another bite of rare steak. So was the food. She was poking at her breast of chicken, scattering bits of rice pilaf around her plate and generally violating most of the rules of etiquette that she and Julie drilled into their clients. Taking what comfort he could from her obvious agitation, he nodded his head, indicating that she had his full attention.

Brenna had been talking nonstop since taking her first sip of the golden wine, waiting impatiently each time the waiter paused at the table and picking up where she'd left off as soon as he'd gone. "So you see how totally wrong last night was," she summed up briskly, looking at him with expectant green eyes, obviously hoping that he'd take her words at face value. "This thing between us simply won't work."

"Bull."

Brenna waited. When he just kept working on his steak, she said, "Bull? That's it? I've talked for a solid hour and that's all you have to say?"

Kane looked up, meeting her indignant gaze. "I'm trying to keep it polite. I don't know where you dreamed up this fantasy of yours, but it sounds deadly. None of us have complete control over our lives, there are always outside factors involved. Besides, what does that have to do with us?"

"Everything!"

"And despite your impassioned statement to the contrary, you are one hell of a loving woman," he continued forcibly. Nudging his plate to one side, he stared across the width of the table, holding her gaze with the force of his. "Lady, I was in bed with you last night. I know."

Brenna closed her eyes against the satisfaction on his lean face. "Did you listen to a thing I said?" she demanded finally, not even trying to conceal her exasperation. "Or are you being deliberately obtuse? You've misinterpreted practically every word I said."

Brenna's brows drew together as she frowned at Kane. She was doing a lot of that tonight, he thought, nodding at the waiter hovering nearby to remove the plates. It was a sure sign that the conversation wasn't going the way she planned it. This was a woman with a head full of plans, he reflected grimly. She had plans for moving to a larger office, plans for the home she eventually wanted to buy on the outskirts of town, plans for her social and professional life. And none of them included him.

She was also nervous. Trying like hell not to show it, but the signs were there in the too-straight line of her back and the way she fiddled with the long-stemmed glass. When her gaze met his, her sea-green eyes flaring with resentful wariness, Kane was reminded of the first time he had seen her. She had been talking to several of his business acquaintances at the Santa Barbara conference, and he'd stayed at a distance, casually taking stock of her. A cool, leggy blonde who talked with her eyes rather than her body. Both were worth a second glance. Her hair was shoulder length, brushed back from her face, several tendrils escaping, touching full lips that liked to smile. The next instant, when the sound of her low tantalizing laugh drifted his way, he'd moved nearer.

Even before he'd closed in and introduced himself, he'd decided that he wanted the unconscious sensuality of her smile directed at him. Exclusively. At the same time, he made several other discoveries: his feelings weren't in the least casual, he had a definite streak of possessiveness and she didn't have the faintest idea that the men around her were all but pawing the ground. That either said something about her awareness of her own sexuality or about the muting effect of polite society on the current generation of corporate sharks.

When he cut her out of the pack and settled her at a restaurant, her back to the rest of the room, he learned that Brenna was single and owned half of a flourishing little company called A Touch of Class. She and her partner were etiquette and media consultants to executives who were climbing the corporate hierarchy and suddenly finding themselves in the public spotlight. She lived and worked in San Diego where his company was based.

That was going to make things a hell of a lot easier, one part of his mind registered, while the rest of him zeroed in on the reluctant way she responded to personal questions. It took him a minute to realize that the cool little lady executive was reserved, if not actually shy. He suspected she also had an inner fire that would burn the socks off the right man. It was buried—so deeply that she didn't even seem aware of it—but it was there. And he, Kane Matthews, was the right man.

Before Brenna had made a dent in her pasta salad, he knew that she would end up in his bed. He also knew he wouldn't rush her. When they came together—there was no question in his mind that they would—she would want it as much as he did. But at the moment he was dealing with a lady whose smile promised little in the way of intimacy, one who made no bones about her policy of drawing a distinct line between her personal and private lives. To cross it would take a man who was as prudent as he was persistent.

He decided that the dividing line merited some thought. Had a man been responsible for it? he wondered idly. Possibly. If so, the lesson learned had been a hard one, he reflected, because every word she uttered painted a picture of a woman who was in charge of her life and would neither turn the running of it over to anyone else nor accept any outside interference. Interesting.

As soon as they were back in San Diego, he called her about a new office complex opening up. Over lunch they casually discussed the possibility of her relocating there. At dinner they decided it wasn't a wise move. The next day he had another suggestion. And on the next, they reviewed several other options open to her. Before she had time to wonder how he had worked his way into her life, he was firmly entrenched. And for the first time in years, he had pushed aside the impatience that was so much a part of him and set about courting a woman, meeting her on her own turf. She wanted cool? He gave her cool. She wanted contained and restrained? That's exactly what she got. What he got was a lot of cold showers.

And that's how it had been until last night. He had made few demands, and her response to his carefully casual kisses never once reflected the unconscious hunger that occasionally darkened her eyes. Until last night.

"Why did you do it?" Brenna demanded suddenly, pulling him away from his thought and bringing his gaze back to her face.

"Do what?"

"Lie to me."

"Brenna," he warned evenly, "there are probably a lot of things you can accuse me of, but lying isn't one of them."

"Prevaricating, then. Departing from the truth. Whatever you want to call it. You're nothing at all like the man you pretended to be for six weeks. Don't you think you could call that lying?" she prodded, shifting uneasily beneath his enigmatic gaze.

"Nope." He reached over and captured her small, restless hand in his.

She tugged and he tightened his grip. "Your peculiar brand of logic escapes me," she grumbled in exasperation, torn between the struggle to retrieve her hand and the pull of his gaze.

He shrugged. "There's no big mystery to it. We all have a few characteristics that we don't use as often as others, but not using them doesn't mean that we don't have them. For six weeks I was the most patient and self-controlled man you've probably ever been around, so how can you say that I was living a lie? It isn't easy to pretend; in fact, it's almost impossible. If I didn't have at least a kernel of those traits, I would have blown it in the first ten minutes. It was simply a case of being whatever the situation called for. You should understand that."

"What do you mean, 'whatever the situation called for'?" she demanded. "Why couldn't you just be yourself?"

"I was," he repeated, opting to ignore the first question.

Brenna looked upward for a long moment, clearly pleading for help from a higher source. When none was forthcoming, she sighed and said, "Tell me another one."

"It was very character building," he assured her with a swift grin.

Eying Kane cautiously, she added belatedly, "And what do you mean, I should understand? I've always been honest with you."

"Have you?"

"Absolutely."

"Lady, your whole life is a lie." Kane felt the slim fingers beneath his own curl into a fist as temper flashed in her eyes.

Brenna took a calming breath. It didn't help. "Would you like to explain that?" she asked finally. When her gaze tangled with his, she wished she hadn't pushed the issue.

"Where do you want to start?" he drawled. "With eyes that show you're hungry for my touch? With lips that moved over mine, making the damnedest sounds of pleasure I've ever heard? With a body that shivered with delight when I touched it?'' He ignored her sharp gasp of outrage. "Or with a briefcase, suits and neat little pumps, the uniform of the lady executive?''

Brenna jerked her hand out of his grasp. If any humor had existed in the situation, it was gone. "I own a business,'' she reminded him coldly. "I dress professionally.''

He nodded in agreement. "Sure you do. We all do. That's one aspect. What about the rest of it?''

"*What* rest?''

"Are you one dimensional? Isn't there anything in your life besides your business? Have you buried your feelings so deep that you don't even admit they exist, just so it's easier to control things?''

Brenna looked out the window, escaping the pull of his demanding gray eyes. Was it asking too much to be allowed to plan her own life, to have some say in the matter of how involved she became with a man? She slid a quick glance at the set expression of Kane's face. Apparently it was. Damn the man, she thought, ignoring the appalling sense of loss creeping over her as she contemplated the future without him. But if he couldn't understand that she didn't want to be swallowed up by him, that she needed the freedom to make her own decisions, then it was better to do exactly what she had intended to do: end things right now.

Turning back to him, she said quietly, "I know exactly what kind of woman I am.''

"Good.''

Kane's slight smile was so lazy and dangerous that she didn't trust it one bit. For some reason it made her think of a great cat about to pounce. She tilted her head and stared narrowly at him. There wasn't anything about her comment that should have made him look like that.

He reached for her hand again and thoughtfully stroked one of her pink oval fingernails with the pad of his thumb, drawing her gaze to their hands—his larger, stronger and tanner than hers, with a sprinkling of dark hair. A hand that knew how to bring overwhelming pleasure to a woman. To her. His voice brought her back to the present with a jolt.

"Yes, I suppose you do. Everything about your house shows it. You don't enjoy anything that's passive and lifeless," he told her. "Your plants, for instance."

Brenna blinked. What on earth did the plants have to do with anything?

"You can't keep your hands off them."

"So?" she asked cautiously, feeling as though she was entering a dark room, groping her way through a network of cobwebs.

"Every time you pass them, you reach out and stroke them."

Stroke. She had the impression that he'd selected the word with great care. Not touch, not handle. Stroke. He'd deliberately invested the word with sensuality, and in the pause that followed, her heightened awareness warned her that he wasn't through.

"I touch them," she admitted slowly, willing to go just so far. "I take great pleasure doing so."

"Your place is full of beautiful things, and they all remind me of you."

"Of me?" she repeated, feeling like a straight man in a comedy routine. But there wasn't anything funny about the situation and not a bit of humor in the tenacious man across from her.

"They're subtle and very sensual."

The flame of the candle was reflected in her wide, startled eyes, along with a distinct touch of alarm. "I'm not like that, Kane! Not at all."

He leaned back and regarded her with genuine interest. "Exactly how do you see yourself?" he asked curiously.

Gripping the fragile stemmed glass in her hands, Brenna inhaled, savoring the delicate bouquet of the wine while she stalled. The thought came to her that she didn't spend a lot of time thinking about herself—at least not analytically. She ran an absent finger around the rim of her glass before taking a sip.

"I lucked out genetically," she said finally. "I inherited good bones and skin from some rather attractive ancestors. Other than that, I'm not much different from anyone else. I like things orderly and stable and I don't like surprises that turn my life upside down. I'm hardworking, practical and prefer reading to watching a lot of television. All in all," she finished with a small shrug, "I guess I'm a fairly dull person."

Kane's deep laugh was a wholly amused, totally male sound. "You aren't serious."

"Oh, yeah, I forgot that part," she said, the corner of her mouth lifting briefly at his genuine amusement. "I do tend to take things rather seriously." Like last night, she thought suddenly, when his touch had made her forget caution and ignore the hard lessons she'd learned over the years.

Her eyes darkened at the memory. His shaken whisper calling to her in the way that men had called their women from the beginning of time. *I knew you'd look like this. Beautiful...golden...hot...sweet. Hungry...for me. Yes. That's it, honey. Touch me... Yes! God, yes!*

"Brenna?"

She blinked at the sound of his voice. Then, remembering what she'd been saying, she leaned forward, her eyes wide with entreaty, trying one last time to make him understand. Blinking away the memory of his hands settling on her waist, drawing her against the heat of his body, she said, "Kane, you've simply got to understand that last night was a mistake. A very big one. I'm not an impulsive person, I just don't go around *doing* things like that."

"You mean I was an exception?"

She eyed his bland expression with misgivings. He looked far too pleased with himself. "You were a mistake," she repeated grimly.

The lines of humor faded from his face as if they had never existed. "Mistake or not, it happened, and there's no way in hell that you can pretend it didn't."

"I can try," she began, in an effort, to stop him. From the look on his face, she didn't think she wanted to hear the rest of what he had to say. She was right.

"That's where we differ. I'm hoping for a rerun, as soon and as often as possible."

Brenna studied the man across from her. What Kane Matthews lacked in good looks, he more than made up for in sheer masculine force. His lean, angular face was strong; its only softness lay in his long, dark lashes and the vertical lines etched in his cheeks, lines that were deep and devastating on the rare occasions when he smiled. Intelligence and thirty-three years of experience gleamed in his cool, gray eyes. The strength of his large-boned body looked impressive and, unfortunately for her, his determination was just as daunting.

Brenna was suddenly aware of the heavy silence that had fallen between them. A quick look at Kane told her that he wasn't in the least affected by it; he was simply waiting for her next objection so that he could calmly swat it aside.

The whole situation was getting on her nerves. Just that morning she had told herself he was a reasonable man. She had been convinced that all she had to do was find the right words to make him understand that he couldn't come crashing into her life, that her plans didn't include his frank sexual approach to life. Well, she had exhausted her vocabulary and he still hadn't gotten the message. Only a flaming optimist would still consider persuasion a viable option. A sensible person would run for her life!

The problem was, she acknowledged ruefully, that if she were fool enough to run, he'd go after her for the sheer thrill of the chase. And he'd thrive on the challenge. Brenna sighed. With her limited options, she was back to reasoning. Ah, well, why not give it one more try? At this point, she didn't have anything to lose. With sudden resolution, she swallowed the remaining wine in her glass and set the stemmed glass carefully on the table.

Before she could muster her forces, Kane's gaze moved from her fingers, which were still gripping the glass, to her face. "Why are you so hell-bent on keeping me out of your life?"

Brenna blinked at the direct attack. There were several truthful answers to that question, she reflected, knowing she would give none of them. Most were too revealing, others he wouldn't accept.

"What happened last night?" he prodded.

Her shrug was an almost imperceptible movement of her shoulders. "Nothing." *Everything. For the first time in my life I understood my mother. And I realized how easy it would be to follow in her footsteps.*

His eyes narrowed at the single, maddening word. "Don't you think your family would approve of me?"

Brenna looked out the window at the receding waves below. When she finally turned back to him, he was waiting. He had a look on his face that convinced her he would sit there until midnight if he had to.

"Which part of my family?" she wondered aloud. "My father? He died when I was ten. My mother? She lives in Arizona with my third stepfather. My grandmother in San Francisco?" She tilted her head and considered him thoughtfully. "Gram would definitely approve."

Kane kept his gaze locked on Brenna's expressive face. With a little luck, he might just find the key to his elusive lady. But he could also blow the whole thing, he decided after another look at her pensive expression. She looked as though she already regretted being so frank and planned to start backpedaling at any second. Masking his intense interest, he asked idly, "What happened after your father died?"

She hesitated. "I went to live with Gram."

"Why?"

Because my mother fell in love with a painter and went off with him to "find" her artistic self. "My mother remarried," she said carefully, "and we all agreed that the newlyweds needed some time to themselves."

His eyes met hers over the rim of his glass. "How long did you stay with your grandmother?"

She shrugged again. "Until I went away to college."

Kane's brows rose. "You never went back to your mother?"

"I didn't get along with her next husband," she said lightly. That was the gardener, and her mother had been up to her neck in mildewed roses and landscaping classes.

"And number three?"

"He's nice enough," she said calmly. The sculptor. And her mother was with him in an artists' colony throwing pottery, convinced that she was the next national treasure in the art world.

"Did it bother you?"

"Not being with my mother? Sometimes. But Gram is a great believer in shaping your own destiny and she was a wonderful role model." She laughed softly, her eyes soft with remembrance. "On my fourteenth birthday she gave me a box of books, the self-help kind." Soothed by the rhythm of the waves, scarcely aware of his silence, she spoke softly. "It was quite an assortment, ranging from positive thinking to Zen."

Kane's long fingers moved on the stem of the crystal glass. He nodded, concentrating on the pale, swirling liquid.

"A lot of it went over my head, but enough didn't. I picked a little of this and a bit of that. Mainly I learned that we're each responsible for creating our own inner strength and direction." She nodded slowly. "I think that was a real turning point in my life."

Kane nodded, keeping his eyes on the amber wine. He mentally filled in the blanks of Brenna's sparse narrative. A ten-year-old kid who had lost both her father and mother, floundering to rebuild her life. No wonder control was right up on top of her priority list. He was willing to bet his new Mercedes that it hadn't taken her long to get the hang of her new philosophy and start building.

And once she moved out on her own, there had probably been no stopping her. She had designed her life in nice, predictable little blocks and that was exactly the way she wanted it to remain. Earlier, she had made it quite clear that there was no place in her scheme of things for disturbing surprises. And there was definitely no place for a man who challenged her own beliefs—especially one who demonstrated that her sensuality could burn her precious peace and tranquillity to cinders.

His face darkened at the conclusion he had drawn and two hours later, seated in Brenna's living room, his mood hadn't lightened appreciably.

Brenna was curled up in a corner of the couch, her white skirt and green sweater a strong contrast to the apricot velvet fabric. Kane lounged comfortably in a nearby chair watching her. He had taken off his jacket, loosened his tie and rolled his shirtsleeves to his forearms. In an attempt to break the deepening silence, she asked, "What brought on that wry expression?" As far as she could see, there had been little enough to smile over that evening.

"You. You're such a little sensualist, and you're totally blind to that side of yourself."

Shifting restlessly at his uncompromising tone, Brenna wished she'd had the good sense to keep her mouth closed.

"But you've spent the evening telling me that I have the wrong impression of you, so let's see if I've got it straight. You're reasonably satisfied with the way you look, intelligent, quiet and a bit dull. Am I right so far?"

Brenna's eyes narrowed at the drawled words. But to be fair, he was repeating her earlier description almost word for word. It just sounded ... different when he said it. A curt nod was her only reply.

"Good. You don't like surprises and you're not impulsive. You're most comfortable when you call the shots and you prefer your relationships on the cool side. As far as your future is concerned, you plan to find a nice, placid man, drift into a nice placid marriage, have children and live happily ever after in a nice, placid neighborhood." Dark brows rose in inquiry. "How am I doing?"

Everything that Brenna had learned about self-control went sailing out the window. "You really are a bastard, aren't you?" she breathed, fighting the impulse to throw something at him. "You make me sound like a self-satisfied idiot!"

"Those aren't *my* words," he pointed out evenly. "I don't see you that way at all."

Eyeing the deepening creases in his cheeks with suspicion, she said rashly, "Then, by all means, tell me how *you* would describe me."

Kane's smile was a warning in itself. "I thought you'd never ask." His eyes gleamed with satisfaction and in that split second she knew she had fallen smack into the trap he had waited all night to spring.

"Never mind," she said hastily, already regretting her impulsive words, "I've changed my mind."

"The businesswoman is one savvy lady, one I'd want on my side of the bargaining table," he murmured, his gaze making a deliberate sweep over her still form. "But lately, I admit that I've been concentrating on getting a certain wide-eyed blonde into my bed. Then when I did and found that she had skin like silk, breasts that—"

"Kane!"

"—were made to fit my hands, and long, smooth legs that wrapped around me—"

"*Kane*!"

He gave a slight shrug, his eyes gleaming wickedly as they studied her pink face. "So, you see," he said mildly, "I rate you right up there around spectacular."

"That's enough!"

He surprised her by giving a nod of agreement. "Okay, let's talk about surprises. Admittedly you had more than your share of upsetting ones when you were a kid, but someone should have taught you that they can also be fun."

"Look—" Brenna had time for just the one word before he swept on.

"What really concerns me is this passion you have for control. A certain amount of it isn't bad, but sometimes you have to give a little."

"Like you do, I suppose."

"Oh, there's one more thing."

"Only one?" she murmured sarcastically.

"This idea you have that you're not a sensual woman."

"Kane," she warned, "don't start that again."

"Just look around this room," he commanded. "Everything in it appeals to the senses. The fabrics cry out to be touched." Brenna laced her fingers together to stop them from stroking the soft velvet. "You have fresh, fragrant flowers in the room, not silk or plastic. The colors are bright and inviting, and what do you have to seduce the ear? Wind chimes. Admit it, Brenna, you take great pleasure in every one of these things."

"I never said I didn't," she retorted angrily. "I simply said that, sexually speaking, I'm not the type of woman who...does what I did last night."

From the gleam of amusement in his eyes and the deepening creases in his cheeks, she knew he wouldn't have anything helpful to say so she rushed on. "And since I'm not going to risk being put in the same situation again, I'm telling you that it's over, finished. I don't want to see you anymore." There. She'd done it. Once and for all. *Again*.

Three

———

You have to," Kane said calmly. "At least until we get all our other business taken care of."

Brenna stiffened. "*What* other business?"

"How soon we forget," he murmured. "I've offered to help you find a new office, remember? And to make sure that you qualify for a small business loan."

Closing her eyes and counting slowly, a part of Brenna noted that her sense of heady relief had dissipated as quickly as it had come. Damn it, didn't he ever give up? Dealing with Kane was as aggravating as trying to gain a foothold on a muddy bank. Every time she thought she'd made some progress, she slipped right back to where she had started.

"What on earth are you talking about?" she demanded blankly. The expression on his face simply wasn't to be trusted, she decided. He looked entirely too pleased with himself.

"The appointments," he said helpfully.

She said through clenched teeth, "*What* appointments?"

He held up one finger. "My realtor. She told me she found a couple of interesting possibilities for you." Another finger joined the first. "And my accountant has drawn up some preliminary figures for you."

"I don't believe this!" Brenna looked at him in amazement. "We've *talked* about these things, but that was all. Are you telling me that you actually scheduled meetings for me?"

His smile said it was a negligible thing but entirely his pleasure. "It was no trouble at all," he told her, getting to his feet.

"Kane!"

His brows shot up. "Or did I misunderstand? I thought that's what you wanted."

She shot him a suspicious look. They *had* talked about it, true. But that's all they had done. She hadn't asked him for anything. At least she didn't think so. At this point, though, she wasn't sure of anything.

"Oh, there's one last thing," he said as she opened her mouth to protest. "How much time will we need to work on that TV interview?"

Good God. Her mouth snapped closed. How could she have forgotten that? Automatically she picked up his jacket and moved toward the front door. Kane had been asked to appear on a television show for an in-depth discussion of the computer software field and had come to her for help.

"We have a contract," he reminded her.

"I haven't forgotten," she assured him, lying with aplomb.

Kane picked up their empty cups and headed for the kitchen. Looking back over his shoulder, he said, "I know how busy you've been and haven't wanted to rush you. That's why I didn't mention it earlier."

"And if I believe that, there's some kind soul waiting in San Francisco to sell me a big red bridge," she muttered to the back of his head.

He disappeared around the corner, and she heard the sound of water running in the sink. When he reappeared, he had a towel draped over his broad shoulder. "I know I've been dragging my heels on this thing, but for the past few days I've been watching the show. I know a couple of his recent guests. They're interesting, articulate people, and several of them have come away looking like real jerks. I'm going to need help," he said simply, "and you're the best around."

Disarmed, she automatically extended his jacket when he offered her the damp towel. He bent his head and dropped a swift, light kiss on her lips. When he stepped out on the small wooden porch into the cool June night, she followed.

"Get some rest," he ordered lightly, the deepening creases in his cheeks distracting her. "You didn't get much sleep last night, and—"

"Kane!"

He smiled down at her, enjoying the flustered glare of outrage, the warning that flickered within the green depths of her eyes.

Just as he reached the bottom of the small flight of stairs, she urgently repeated his name. He stopped, waiting. He hadn't expected her to give up so easily. Persistence seemed to rank right up there with her need to control things.

When he looked up at her, she made one last attempt. "Why don't you let me ask Julie to work with you? She's good and..." Her voice faded when he just stood there, shaking his head.

"No." Kane knew his voice was too rough. He also knew that unless she moved away from the light pouring out the door, framing her slim body, it was going to get a lot rougher. There was nothing provocative about her green knit sweater and summer-white skirt, he decided objectively, wrapping his hand around the wrought iron rail to keep himself from going back up the short flight of stairs. It was simply that she, in whatever she wore, tied him up in knots. The silver hoops of her pierced earrings glimmered as they twisted and turned in the light. Her fair hair fell in a casual tumble, softly framing her face. A classy style for a classy lady.

But when it came right down to it, he preferred her as she had been last night. Her pale hair spread over his pillow like a splash of golden silk. Her bare legs tangled with his as her hands moved over him like warm honey, her eyes wide with sensual promise—a young Eve discovering her feminine power. Fighting the urge to go back, pick her up and carry her to the nearest bed, he said instead, "Don't worry, honey, we'll work it out. I'll call you sometime before noon."

Turning away before he changed his mind, he walked to his car and opened the door. As he inserted his key in the ignition, he made a mental note to call both the realtor and accountant first thing in the morning. They'd have to scramble something together just in case she decided to take him up on his offer.

The gunmetal Mercedes slid silently down the broad avenue, merged with heavier traffic around Balboa Park and turned north on the freeway, heading toward Del Mar.

Driving automatically, Kane frowned recalling the look on Brenna's face earlier that evening when she'd accused him of deceiving her, when she said she didn't know the man she had been with the night before. He had news for her— she didn't know much about the woman he'd been with, either. The lines of his face relaxed and one corner of his hard mouth curved up. It would be his distinct pleasure to help her get acquainted with them both. Intimately.

Brenna slumped against the doorjamb, watching the dark car ease down the street. "Damn." How did he do it? Annoyance ran a close second to genuine bewilderment. So far, in this crazy game they seemed to be playing, her score was a solid zip. When his taillights were out of sight, she went back inside and closed the door behind her, returning the dish towel to the kitchen and absently rinsing the few dishes left on the counter.

How could things get so out of hand in a matter of twenty-four hours? she wondered, thinking back to the night before. She had driven to his house, anticipating the steak he had promised her. They had planned to celebrate the balmy weather by using the barbecue on the deck.

She liked his house on the hill. Since land was at a premium in Del Mar, the house itself covered most of the lot and was built up rather than out, with a deck on the second floor running the whole length of the side overlooking the ocean. Inside it was pleasantly turned upside down, with bedrooms and an office on the first level; a kitchen, dining room and combination living room and den sprawled on the second, separated from the deck by glass walls. The living room, with its gleaming wood floors and sturdy, masculine furniture, was unexpectedly inviting. The rich, soft colors of a Persian rug enhanced the classic warmth of the light, stone fireplace and black slate hearth.

The kitchen had oak cabinets and soft yellow walls. All in all, she had enjoyed her infrequent visits there.

But last night a new element had been added. It was obvious as soon as he opened the door. By the time he had handed her a drink and led her out to the deck, she realized that somewhere within Kane's hard body was a coiled spring about to snap. It made her distinctly edgy. As she set the outdoor table, his charged, silvery gaze kept sliding over her until she wanted to scream. Instead she dropped silverware and tripped over shadows.

What she was dealing with here, she decided as she sat across from him and tried to concentrate on her steak, was pure, unadulterated, barely controlled hunger. Male hormones on a roll, real caveman stuff.

And it scared the daylights out of her.

While watching him across the table with wary eyes, she considered one of the small ironies of life. Part of her business was teaching budding executives the fine points of etiquette, acquainting them with the rules that separated the civilized from the savage, yet she had managed to become involved with a man who broke rules as easily as most people followed them. More easily, in fact. And if he ran out of other people's rules, he made his own—which was exactly what he seemed to be doing right now.

And that's what it all came down to, she had realized with a start. They were on his turf, in his world, playing by his rules. Not only didn't she understand the rules, but she didn't even know how to play the game!

And he was through waiting.

Oddly enough it wasn't until that moment, when the thought hit her like a bolt of lightning, that she realized that was exactly what he had been doing for the past six weeks. Waiting. One quick glance at his hard face and direct gaze confirmed her theory. He'd held off just long enough for her to be curious, tempted, drawn by kisses that promised something more, wanting those promises fulfilled. In other words, he'd waited until she had walked into the trap.

Brenna wasted about ten seconds regretting the loss of the man she thought she had found, the one who would fit in perfectly with her carefully planned life. For the rest of the meal, she worked on survival. She was still refining her plan when she had helped Kane carry the dishes into the kitchen.

Her job was always a good excuse. She'd tell him—regretfully, of course—that she had to get home and work on a presentation for tomorrow. A new commission. The client had just called and needed her right away. Julie was busy and she had to handle it all by herself. That should do it. Her nod was short and satisfied. She would have been far less complacent if she had noticed the speculative gleam in the gray eyes that followed her around the kitchen.

An hour later, sitting next to him on the dark brown couch, watching the fire he had started when the air had cooled, she was still waiting for the proper moment to haul out her excuse. Every time she opened her mouth, Kane tried to fill it. Coffee? Dessert? A drink?

"Kane," she had begun briskly, only to be brought up short when he gently tugged her closer. His gaze moved over her mouth like a lingering kiss, and he threaded his fingers in her hair, removing the clips that swept it off her face. He had watched it tumble to her shoulders, then reached out and slowly wound a long strand around his hand. Her agitation grew at the frankly possessive expression in his eyes.

"What, love?" he murmured, his lips teasing the sensitive skin behind her ear.

She didn't *know* what, she realized hazily, arching reflexively against his hand as it moved skillfully down her spine—only that everything was changing. His lazy control was fading and her inner alarms were clamoring in warning, telling her that if she wanted to stop him, now was the time! She halfheartedly murmured a protest against his throat when he lifted her, settling her across his thighs.

"I want you, Brenna. I have since the first time I saw you."

Brenna's heavy lashes had lifted at the aggressive statement, and this time she listened to the tolling alarms. There was nothing the least bit lazy about Kane Matthews now. His chest rose and fell as if he had been running, and his eyes made no secret of his hunger.

Telling herself that she should have followed her instincts and given her excuses an hour ago, Brenna had tried to move and found herself caught securely in the curve of his arm. "Kane," she muttered, giving another wiggle, "I think we need to talk." Tension shivered through her when his hand clamped on her thigh, lightly kneading it, removing all possibility of her slipping from his lap.

"Honey," he had said with a trace of dark humor, "you may not have noticed, but that's just about all we've done for the past six weeks."

When his lips had settled on hers in a kiss that curled her toes, Brenna thought of promises. Part of her anticipation before she had arrived had come from the knowledge that she would allow herself to move a step or two closer to the intriguing man whose muted gaze had always promised that he would deliver only what she was prepared to accept. Now a soft moan caught deep in her throat and she shivered, torn between wanting him and astonishment that her need was so great.

"Ah...Kane," she had said, hazily aware of his hand brushing over the buttons at the back of her sundress, of the fabric falling away from her shoulders. Blinking in surprise, her gaze lowered from the taut lines of his face to his hand, just as he released the front catch of her lacy bra, leaving her bare to the waist.

"Oh!"

He didn't even seem to hear her soft gasp. "Don't hide from me, honey," he had said huskily when she instinctively lifted her hands to his. He brushed them aside and looked at her, pleasure evident in his silvery eyes. Then he reached out and deliberately rubbed his thumbs against the beaded tips of her breasts.

A shock wave of urgent need had swept through her, alarming Brenna almost as much as the sudden, predatory look on his face. Never, ever, had a man made her ache so with just a touch. Never had she been so tempted by a man's look of approval.

"Don't," she had whispered shakily, covering his hands with hers, then drawing in another sharp breath. All she had succeeded in doing was to keep him exactly where he wanted to be while the tips of her breasts nudged his cupped palms.

"You're blushing," Kane had informed her, shifting to hold her more securely.

He sounded surprised, she had thought, exasperation blending for a moment with anxiety. His absorbed study of her wasn't helping, she decided, feeling heat wash over her from her breasts to her eyebrows. And why on earth wouldn't she be blushing? It wasn't as if she made a habit of lying naked in—

"What?" she demanded, not believing her ears.

Kane had trailed a finger from the delicate hollow in her throat to the satiny area between her breasts, watching with absorbed pleasure as the dark pink tips hardened even more. "I said," he repeated obediently, "that there's no need for you to be embarrassed. None at all. Because you're beautiful. And besides, you belong to me, so it's all right."

Indignant green eyes had met possessive gray ones.

"No, Kane," she said urgently, "that's not true." Watching his expression harden, she swallowed and, before she lost her nerve, added hastily, "Nobody owns—!"

Her words were stopped by his kiss, that time a deliberate, dominating kiss. And that time, when his mouth closed over hers, there was none of the restraint she associated with him, no lazy patience. Instead he opened her mouth with his and drew her full lower lip between his teeth, holding her captive until he felt her go very still in his arms. When he was certain he'd made his point, he had released her, his tongue gently stroking her lip, then seeking the warmth within her mouth. His hands moved down to her hips, cupping her rounded bottom, and he tugged her closer, holding her against his hard warmth.

Brenna had stiffened, stunned by his uncharacteristic aggression, her hands braced against his chest. He hadn't hurt her, she admitted to herself, trying and failing to work her arms between them. But he'd definitely gotten his point across. What she should do, she thought uncertainly, was stop him right now. But she doubted if she could. And to be absolutely honest, she wasn't sure she wanted to. Later she would. In a little while. But not now. The man kissing her was a far cry from the cool, unruffled Kane Matthews who would fit quite nicely into her life. But even as she had considered the difference, her traitorous body told her what she already knew: which*ever* man he was, she ached for his touch. A soft moan, deep in her throat, told him as well.

Responding to her small cry, Kane deepened the kiss, imprinting his taste and touch on her, seeming to take great pleasure in her soft, hungry murmurs. And deep within her, one part of Brenna's mind registered the fact that while he wasn't behaving anything like the imperturbable man she'd known for the past six weeks, Kane was still in perfect control. He obviously wanted her, was apparently determined to have her, but he would never hurt her. She wasn't quite certain how she knew that, but she did. Shivering, she thought that it was a good thing because she had never before been so vulnerable with a man.

Applying one last, gentle nip to her lip, Kane raised his head and looked down at her flushed face. "Aren't you curious, Brenna?" he had whispered huskily, bringing her hand to the top button of his shirt. "You've never once put your hands on me. I want to be touched . . . like this." He bent his head and stroked her tightly beaded nipple with the tip of his tongue.

Brenna's breath hissed between her teeth and she cried softly as liquid fire raced through her body, creating unbearable tension.

"Touch me, Brenna." The husky whisper had gone from a taut demand to soft encouragement as her fingers fumbled at the buttons then slowly eased into the curling mat of hair covering his chest, tracing a path over the broad, flat muscles. "I've ached for you to do that since the first time I saw you."

Drawn by the need he made no effort to conceal, absorbed in her tactile exploration, Brenna barely heard his words. While one hand continued its quest, the other slid to a stop over his thudding heart, felt the heat blazing from him, the faint dampness beneath the springy hair. Kneading him delicately with her fingertips, she had remembered his question. Yes, she was curious, she thought dazedly. No, that was a pale, anemic word to express what she felt. Her need to touch him was overwhelming.

Barely able to breathe, Kane had looked down at the absorbed expression on her face. Relief and triumph surged through him. She didn't know it yet, but she wanted him every bit as much as he needed her. Impatiently he tore off his shirt and tossed it to the end of the sofa then drew her closer, groaning as he fit her soft body against him.

Lost in a new world of discovery, Brenna had wrapped her arms around him, caressing his lean back, pausing briefly at his shoulders then stopping altogether when, with an impatient movement, Kane tugged her sundress down past her hips and dropped it on the floor. She looked down, blinking. All that remained of her clothes was a silky scrap of fabric at her hips.

"Don't you dare quit now," he ordered, half amused and half alarmed by her disconcerted expression. "Don't even think about it."

She had tilted her head against his shoulder, looking up through her lashes. "I couldn't," she admitted, turning her face into his neck and touching her lips to the strong, rapid pulse beating there. And that was the truth, simple and awesome as it was. There was no turning back.

Once she had cast her last doubt aside, Brenna was amazed at how natural it was to touch him. Sliding her arms around his neck, she had tangled her fingers in his hair, luxuriating in the dark pelt, drawing him closer, tempting him with her parted lips, encouraged by his muffled groans of pleasure. Her small smile was purely feminine when she felt the last of her clothes join the dress on the floor.

With an ease that stunned her, Kane had shifted Brenna beneath him, his body settling on her with sensual deliberation, carrying her down into the cushions. She pressed against his taut length, aware of his need and exulting in the heady feeling of feminine power that washed over her. Her hand worked down his flat stomach, fumbled with his belt, and came to a halt, as she muttered discontentedly.

A chuckle sounded near her ear, one replete with male satisfaction. Kane dropped one last kiss at the corner of her mouth then surged to his feet. He tore off his clothes, scattering them on the floor along with hers.

Curled contentedly on the sofa, her palms absently rubbing the soft woven fabric, Brenna had watched him with unabashed pleasure. He was powerfully muscled, and deeply tanned from his head to his large feet. Silhouetted against the firelight, he was beautiful. He was also magnificently aroused, she reflected complacently, feeling intensely feminine. Ignoring the small inner voice that informed her she was reacting in a manner totally inconsistent with her normal behavior, she sighed but never even thought of looking away.

Kane tossed some pillows on the rug in front of the fireplace and turned to her. Effortlessly picking her up, he grinned down at her and admitted, "I have an irresistible urge to see you by firelight." Going down on one knee, he had settled her on the carpet. He stared down at her for a long, tense moment. Then with a soft groan, he sat next to her, one hand at her hip, the other carefully fanning her hair across the green satin pillow.

"You're so beautiful," he muttered thickly, watching the flickering amber flames reflected in her languid eyes. "You were made to be seen by firelight. It turns you to gold."

Caught between the fire in the stone cavern behind her and the one blazing within the man at her side, Brenna had simply stared up at him, twisting restlessly beneath his stroking hand. "Kiss me, Kane," she whispered, reaching up to touch his mouth with her fingertips.

"Everywhere," he promised.

A series of soft, breathless cries spilled into the room as he rained kisses over her body. When his tongue curled around her taut nipple, tension shuddered through her and spiraled higher and higher as he traced a path of slow, hot kisses down past the soft curve of her stomach, then lower to the sweet, silky juncture of her thighs. Reality became a fantasy of tangled limbs and branding kisses. Shimmering pleasure leaped through her body, building, escalating time and again. And each time he soothed her, touching and easing the unbearable tension, only to begin the incredible sequence again.

"Kane," she had cried, clutching his shoulders, her nails leaving a trail of small crescent marks on them. "No more. You're driving me crazy."

"That's exactly what I want," he had muttered fiercely, brushing his lips along her inner thigh.

"No more! Please, I can't stand it!"

With a sudden movement, he wrapped his arms around her and rolled onto his back, taking her with him and settling her along the length of his hard body. His voice was rough with restraint. "Now you can drive me crazy for a while."

Watching her sit up, her knees easing down the sides of his thighs, her hands braced on his chest, Kane absorbed the picture she made: the tumbled golden hair, lips slightly swollen with love, wide green eyes a little startled, shining with sensual curiosity. "If I live to be a hundred, I'll always remember you as you are right now." His voice was a half whisper, reflecting his deep satisfaction.

Brenna took in the dark invitation of his eyes and smiled down at him with a hint of recklessness. "How do I look?"

His hands had moved possessively over her slim legs. "Rumpled, well loved, a bit daring. Utterly delightful. And all mine."

Leaning forward until her breasts brushed softly against the hard muscles of his chest, she had murmured, "That's exactly how I feel." Eyes bright with challenge, she bent and touched her lips to his. Then she sat back and touched his chest, threading her fingers through the springy mat of hair, following its narrowing path to his flat stomach.

Kane moved convulsively beneath her and his large hands clamped around her waist. "I've changed my mind," he said through his teeth. "I'm crazy enough for ten men."

"Kane?" Brenna grabbed at his wrists to steady herself when he lifted and eased her back to the rug. Nudging her legs apart with his knee, he moved between them and gently, slowly—never taking his eyes form her face—sheathed himself in her welcoming softness.

"Kane!" Her breathless cry was filled with pleasure, matching his soft, exultant laugh. The single word was torn from her.

Rhythm and power, heat and desire, sensations she had only dreamed of overwhelmed Brenna. Responding to the unbearable tension, she slid her hands up and wove her fingers through his hair, pulling him closer. Her legs tightened around him as a small, spasmodic tremor began deep within her. It grew in power and intensity until she had gasped, "I *can't . . .*"

"You can, honey," he assured her. "You will."

"*Kane!*" Her voice cracked as her body shuddered in release.

Four

Brenna winced as the memory of her broken cry and Kane's ragged response seemed to echo through the bright kitchen. Moving quickly, she replaced the towel, flicked the light switch and tried to convince herself that she wasn't running away.

Making her way through the small house, securing it for the night, she decided gloomily that her problem definitely wasn't going to be easily solved. Kane Matthews had made one thing clear: he wasn't about to disappear from her life. Nor was he going to let her forget what could properly be labeled as the biggest mistake she had ever made. She was obviously going to have to come up with something brilliant. And soon.

Thirty minutes and a long, hot shower later, she was no nearer to a solution. Wearing only a short cotton nightgown, she padded into the bedroom and dropped down on the bed, tucking a pillow beneath her head. This was the way she began and ended each day. She didn't dignify it by calling it meditation, it was simply a way of clearing her mind. Every morning she considered her schedule, visualizing each appointment, working her way successfully through each encounter.

At night she contemplated the events of the day, sifting through them, giving herself a mental pat on the back for the ones that went as she'd anticipated, figuring out where the others had gone wrong and making adjustments to correct them. It was a fine system, one that usually worked quite well. It put things in perspective and washed away any residual tension. Afterward, she normally closed her eyes and slept the sleep of the just. It wasn't so easy now because, unfortunately, the system hadn't been designed with Kane Matthews in mind. At least not the Kane Matthews who had emerged from his screen of protective coloring last night. He was enough to put a glitch in *any* technique.

Twenty minutes later she sighed in disgust. As far as she could see, her options were dismal. It didn't do a bit of good to tell a man you wouldn't see him anymore if the man didn't listen. It also didn't do any good to walk away if he camped in your office and waited for you. Or to run if he was the type who would enjoy the ensuing chase. It would be far simpler, she decided, if he weren't the type that thrived on challenges.

Brenna stared up at the ceiling, a thoughtful expression on her face. She stayed that way for a long time, wondering at the possibility that had presented itself. It might work. Yes, she decided finally after giving it a great deal of thought, it might work very well. She snapped out the light, and five minutes later she was asleep, a slight smile curving her lips.

* * *

The next morning when she opened her office door, Julie pounced. "Look at this," she demanded, waving with an extravagant gesture to a large, exotic flower arrangement that sat in the middle of Brenna's desk.

Brenna circled it cautiously. "What is it, a man-eating plant? Who's it for?"

Handing her a small white envelope, Julie said, "Your desk, your flowers. If it were on mine, I would have had the card opened already."

Brenna inserted a fingernail beneath the flap and lifted it, blinking down at the succinct message: ANYTHING IS POSSIBLE GIVEN THE PROPER MOTIVATION. There was no signature; it wasn't necessary. Only one man she knew had the massive self-assurance to send such a declaration.

Julie moved behind her and peered over her shoulder. "Ah," she breathed, "a cryptic message from an unknown admirer. What a great way to start the day. Do we know who it's from?"

"Three guesses," Brenna said. He sounded awfully confident, she reflected, staring down at the card. With reason, she supposed. His memories of her response to him probably hadn't left much room for doubt.

"Kane?"

"Bingo."

"What does he mean?" she asked with the frankness of an old friend. "What's possible?"

"Getting me back in bed," Brenna said absently. Kane certainly knew how to capture one's attention, she decided while contemplating the sweeping floral arrangement that consisted of a giant protea, ti leaves and brilliant anthuriums.

"*Back* in bed?"

Julie's voice managed to be quietly astonished even as it vibrated with disbelief and anticipation. Her words drew Brenna's gaze from the fuzzy evergreen shrub to Julie's expectant face. Her friend's hazel eyes were wide with amused curiosity.

"Oh, hell." Brenna's tone was full of self-disgust. Julie was like one of those TV sleuths who built entire cases on a single, careless word. There wouldn't be a moment's peace until she got to the core of the matter.

"Back?"

Brenna glanced once more at the card before slipping it into the envelope. Knowing it was useless, she tried anyway. "Forget it," she mumbled, moving behind the protective bulk of her desk.

"Back?" Julie insisted, leaning in the doorway and refusing to budge. "Come on, my friend, give."

Brenna sighed sharply and dropped down into the gray executive chair. "I already did, night before last," she admitted morosely, frowning suspiciously as the broad ti leaves swayed and seemed to move closer.

"You're kidding!"

Brenna looked at Julie's stunned expression and slowly shook her head.

"You're serious?"

This time, Brenna's head move up and down.

"You're telling me that you . . ."

Brenna nodded encouragingly when Julie appeared to be stuck.

"and Kane are . . ."

"Lovers," she said baldly. It was the first time she had admitted it. "Were," she amended hastily when she realized the extent of her admission.

"I don't believe it!"

"Why not?" Brenna asked reasonably. "You've been telling me that Kane is the type who takes what he wants. You've obviously been expecting it, so why the surprise?"

Julie frowned. "I don't know. Sure, I expected him to pounce, but I didn't really think he'd get away with it. But if he did," she said slowly, studying her friend's face with narrowed eyes, "why was he here yesterday at the crack of dawn looking like he had chewed on a few nails for breakfast?"

"He, uh, didn't like the note I left him," Brenna admitted reluctantly.

"Ah." Julie nodded in satisfaction.

Brenna scowled. "Ah, what?" She hated it when Julie got that all-knowing expression on her face.

"Ah, you ran out on him."

Brenna nodded. "As fast as I could."

Julie grinned. "Why?"

"Because," Brenna said grudgingly. She would have eventually told Julie the whole story. But it was one thing to tell her willingly, another thing entirely to have the story pulled out of her before she was ready. Damn it, she'd wanted time to ease into it a little.

"But, *why?*" Julie was aghast. "Brenna," she said in a tone one used when explaining basic facts to a simpleton, "Kane isn't your average, run-of-the-mill man. You don't play games with someone like that. He's spectacular, he's..."

"He's not at all what he pretended to be," Brenna said flatly while Julie searched for further superlatives.

"What do you mean?" Then apparently deciding that the question was irrelevant, she protested, "Are you going to hold a little thing like that against him?"

"Yes. For all the good it's doing me."

Julie dropped down into the other chair. "Talk," she commanded. "The whole story. Now."

Brenna explained, keeping the narrative as straightforward as one of her business reports. She didn't spare herself or attempt to evade the issue, but she did do a bit of judicious editing. There was a limit, she reflected, to how much she would share—even with her best friend.

However, no one had ever accused Julie of lacking an imagination, and she was obviously working it overtime. Brenna could almost see her adding flesh and color to the expurgated version she was getting.

"As you can see," Brenna mumbled, "he was, uh, very persuasive." Shifting restlessly, she reflected that putting the events into words had proven to be unexpectedly awkward. And Julie's unblinking fascination wasn't helping. Shrugging, she finished, "So I stayed with him."

Julie picked up a notepad and fanned herself. "Good Lord, I should hope so!"

"You're supposed to be *my* friend," Brenna reminded her dryly. "Whose corner are you in?"

"Yours. But that doesn't mean we always see eye to eye on these things." She let that sink in for a minute then added, "I just have one question."

Brenna regarded her suspiciously.

"Why did you run?"

"Oh, come on, Julie." Moving out from behind the swaying anthuriums, Brenna walked over to the window and glared out at the palm trees lining the street before turning back to her friend. "I've worked too hard, for too many years, to let someone like Kane turn my life upside down."

"Someone like Kane?" Julie repeated softly.

"He has the subtlety of a bulldozer. Besides that, he's a quick-change artist."

Julie's raised brows could have been twin question marks.

"Before I had even gotten used to the idea that there was a man in my life, he whipped off his costume and turned into someone else." She caught Julie's half grin and grimaced. "And there's no doubt about what he is," she concluded in frustration.

"And that is?" Julie asked blandly.

"A shark. He's swimming circles around me, and with each pass he makes, they get smaller and smaller."

"You're scared."

"Darn right."

"What's wrong with falling in love?"

"He's never mentioned the word." Actually she sort of liked the idea, she thought, looking back out at the swaying palm trees. It was simply a matter of finding the right man. An ordinary man, not one like Kane. Not one with his aura of danger, with his passion. Getting involved with Kane would be like falling in love with an avalanche. If she gave in to a man like that, he would take over every aspect of her life.

Julie leaned back in the chair. "He could charm you right out of your socks."

"He already has," she reminded her friend dryly.

"He could add a lot to your life."

"Yeah," Brenna muttered, ignoring the small jolt of anticipation deep within her. "A lot of turmoil."

"What's so bad about that?"

"For you, maybe nothing. You enjoy excitement. But I need tranquillity." She sat back down. "That reminds me, there's something I want to talk over with you."

Julie groaned. "We're not going to discuss master plans again, are we?"

"Nope. Just a small one. But it's not your average, everyday plan and I'm going to need your help, so I'd like a little feedback from you. Got a few more minutes?"

"Judging by the look on your face, I'm going to need more than time. Coffee," she decided, reaching for the pot and jiggling it invitingly over Brenna's cup. "Strong and black. Are we talking plots or plans here? Never mind," she ordered before Brenna could answer, "after what I've heard this morning, nothing will surprise me."

Five minutes later, after listening to Brenna in fascinated silence, she said, "Obviously I was wrong. I'm surprised. Are you crazy? I agree that Kane is the type who thrives on challenge, but that doesn't make him stupid. If anything, I'd say that his intelligence is several notches above average."

Brenna nodded complacently. "Exactly. And right now he thinks that I'm going to keep on seeing him because he's backed me into a corner."

"Instead you're simply going to remove the thrill of the chase by not running?"

"Exactly." Brenna stretched like a satisfied cat.

Julie looked at her dubiously. "Isn't that a bit like leaning into a left hook?"

Brenna's plan, and her resulting euphoria, prompted her to take Kane up on his offer. Two days later, she sat through an extended lunch with Kane and Hugo Harper, his accountant. While the two men pointed out the merits of setting up her own copy center and phone systems, she smiled amiably. When they reminded her that moving her office from her home would drastically increase her fixed expenses, she nodded, an expression of thoughtful consideration drawing her brows together. And when Hugo, a slim man with thinning hair, pulled a sheaf of papers from his briefcase and explained that before making a small business loan the bank would need to examine her budgets and projected revenues, her partnership agreement and tax returns for the last three years, she beamed appreciatively and examined the sample documents he showed her. Not for a moment did she consider remarking that she had already tackled those problems with her own accountant.

While Hugo expanded beneath her smile, Brenna's thoughts returned to her partner. Julie's forte was organization; she kept the office running with the precision of a well-oiled machine. She frankly admitted that her only interest in the financial end of things was the bottom line, so Brenna dealt with banks, realtors and accountants. They each thought they had the best of the deal—which, Brenna decided as she nodded approvingly at Hugo again, was exactly what a partnership should be.

In short, Julie had implicit trust in Brenna's business acumen. It was unfortunate that she didn't have the same faith in her when it came to dealing with men, Brenna reflected while directing a brilliant smile at Kane when she encountered his assessing gaze. Julie didn't believe for a minute that it would be such an easy matter to defuse his predatory instincts, but this time she was wrong. Kane would soon grow tired of a pliant, passive, docile companion. Brenna smiled again at the thought. Julie might not think much of the plan but at least she had agreed to step in and cover for Brenna if it became necessary.

Kane shifted restlessly, staring at Brenna with narrowed eyes. She looked like a cat covered with canary feathers and he didn't trust that innocent expression for a second. She gazed benevolently at Hugo and that made him even more suspicious. No one was that enthralled by an accountant!

His misgivings increased over the next couple of days. Brenna amiably trotted around the city with him and the realtor, dutifully examining one suite of offices after another, until Thelma reluctantly admitted that she had no more to show. Brenna made all the proper noises. She appreciated the time Thelma had spent showing her the properties, she was grateful that Kane had found someone so knowledgeable, they really must let her know if they came across something else.

Kane didn't know if the offices were appropriate or not; he rarely took his wary gaze off Brenna. Probably because of that, he noted that while she was polite and nodded in all the right places, she barely looked at the vacant suites. Her lips went through the motions of smiling, but her eyes reflected a wry, inner amusement that had nothing at all to do with the situation. That particular expression, he decided grimly, was not exactly the one he'd hoped for. What he wanted to see was a growing look of hunger, a realization that she wanted him, couldn't do without his touch. Without him.

Instead he had the distinct feeling that she was biding her time, waiting for something. He spent several long, lonely evenings in front of his fireplace brooding about it, sifting through the possibilities, such as they were. He rejected out of hand the first one that came to mind. She couldn't be waiting for him to get bored and wander away. She wasn't that naive. Or stupid. She couldn't believe that he was playing some adolescent waiting game, complete with time limit and penalties. But eventually, after examining all the other prospects, that was the one he returned to.

Grim faced and swearing, he stalked into the kitchen and pulled a beer out of the refrigerator. Glancing down at a bottle of Zinfandel Blanc he had chilling in there for

Brenna's next visit—whenever that might be—he thought
of her and her crazy notion. Did she honestly think that he
was going to get tired of her? That all she had to do was
play along for a few days, then she'd be home free? He released the door and absently watched it swing closed before he returned to the other room and settled down on the
couch.

Stretching out his legs, he took a long swallow of the
cold beer. The problem he was facing, he thought with a
considering look at what remained in the bottle, was fairly
unique. No, he decided after a moment's contemplation,
scratch "fairly." It was unique. Up until now, most of his
energy had been directed toward his software business. It
was an exploding field and he'd been busting his butt to
stay on the cutting edge. Then he had seen Brenna at the
conference.

Yes, he reflected, replacing his empty bottle with a full
one, unique was the right word. He had never responded
to a woman the way he had to Brenna. As far as that went,
he was doing a lot of things for the first time. He had never
taken one look at a woman, cut her out of the pack, and
kept her away from the predators who prowled hotel lob-
bies at conferences. He had never spent hours devising
ways to make himself necessary to a woman. Until recently, he had never delegated so many tasks at work. He
had never known a woman who tried so hard to discourage him. He had never brought a woman to his home with
the intent of seducing her. He had never made love to a
woman in front of his fireplace. He had never satisfied a
woman the way he had Brenna MacKay. And he had never
responded to another woman the way he did to this one.

Remembering her lying beneath him, clinging to him as
she had the other night, did nothing to reduce the sensual
tension in his body. Still caught in the memory of her hair

sliding like golden silk across his chest, he swore and surged to his feet, moving outside to pace the length of the deck. After a few minutes in the brisk air, he halted and stared down at the lights below, a look of grim determination on his face. Whatever game she was playing, however she expected him to react, it wouldn't work. Come hell or high water, Brenna was coming back to him, to his bed. And regardless of what she thought now, she would do it because she couldn't stay away!

Brenna watched the last image of the mock interview they had just taped fade from the screen, then reached over, switched off the VCR and turned to Kane. For the practice session, she had taken the part of the interviewer and had deliberately thrown a few loaded questions at Kane. "Well, what do you think?"

"You're the pro around here," he replied, leaning back and watching her expressive face. "I think it's more important to know what you think."

"You're better than most," she told him. "You'll have to do some homework, but if we can get together for about three hours, we'll whip you into shape for the Kramer show."

"You sound like you're going to relish every second of it," Kane said with a lazy smile, enjoying her look of anticipation.

"I'm not crazy about the techniques Walton Kramer uses on his guests. I'm going to enjoy watching you pin his ears back. Besides—" her green eyes laughed at him "—it isn't very often that I have control of the situation when we're together. I have to take advantage of every chance I get."

She waited a beat and when he simply looked at her, she rushed on, a little flustered by the expression in his eyes.

"Believe it or not, I had a reason for asking you to wear the same clothes you intend to wear on the program. How do you think you looked?"

"The shirt's wrong."

She nodded. "And the tie. White is a real killer on TV. Switch to a light blue shirt and a red tie and you'll be fine." She checked a small square on a printed list. "Hands," she said briskly, moving down to the next line. "Most people wave them all over the place and it's very distracting. You only did that twice. Since Walton Kramer always has panel members seated at a table, it'll be a snap. Just clasp your hands, rest your forearms on the edge of the table and don't move them."

"Is that all?"

"We're just getting started," Brenna told him serenely, crossing her legs and settling down for a long session. This was her turf; she knew exactly what she was doing. No matter how hard he stared at her legs or let his eyes wander over various parts of her anatomy, she was going to keep him working. Jotting a note on the next line, she said, "Eyes. You were great, you watched me all the time. Do the same with Kramer. Remember, it's the cameraman's job to find you."

Forty minutes later, they were just getting around to the format. "Were you comfortable with the questions?" she asked innocently.

"Of course," he answered, a distinct edge to his voice. "I like it when people throw live grenades at me. What the hell do you mean asking why I don't hire more women? If I'm against minorities?"

"Are you?" she asked, a candid look of inquiry on her face.

Kane drew in a deep breath; his narrowed eyes focused on her guileless expression.

"Don't shoot!" she said, holding up her hand and biting back a laugh. "Okay, it was hitting below the belt, but you've got to be ready for something like that. Kramer is an ambusher, don't ever count on him being sympathetic. That's exactly how he made those people you were telling me about look like jerks. Part of your homework is to think of the ten toughest questions he could throw at you and come up with some answers." After making a notation on the last line, she looked up and said, "That's it for now, unless you have any questions."

He shook his head slowly. "I think you've covered everything. You're good, lady, very good."

"I know." She smiled in quick pleasure. "But it's nice to hear you say so."

He got up and slid his arm around her waist, steering her toward the door. "If I think of anything later, we can talk about it over dinner."

"Umm, sounds good," she said, stepping away from the curve of his arm and bending over to pick up a leather briefcase. "Especially if you were thinking of feeding me a nice, thick steak. But I have to work tonight. Here." She handed him the case. "There are some tapes of Kramer's nastier ambushes in here. Watch how he sets people up. You'll learn a lot."

He stood still in the open doorway, resisting her efforts to usher him out into the main office. "Dinner tomorrow?"

Brenna blinked at the set expression on his hard face. Trying to nudge him through the door was a bit like trying to shove a boulder uphill, she decided. Besides, it wasn't part of her plan to be difficult. "Tomorrow," she promised.

"No late appointments?" he asked.

She shook her head, smiling up at him. "If you promise to feed me, I'm all yours."

Five

Five days later, that rash promise still had the power to make her cringe. Talk about an advanced case of foot-in-mouth disease, she reflected grimly as she pulled up in front of her house, slid out from behind the wheel and locked the car. Kane had had the good sense not to take her literally, but when they were together his eyes followed her with the hungry anticipation of an elegant tomcat watching a tasty mouse and hoping it would fling itself in his path.

She quickly covered the short distance between car and house, placed her briefcase on the floor of her small porch and inserted her key in the lock, suddenly aware of the clamor of the telephone inside. She got it on the seventh ring, her voice breathless. "A Touch of Class, Brenna MacKay speaking."

"Is my timing bad?" Kane sounded abrupt, as if he had been kept waiting for hours. "Are you busy?"

"Hi. No, I just walked in."

"Good. I wanted to catch you before you left for the day."

"And so you did," she said, aware that the unexpected tension had eased from his voice. "But even if you hadn't," she mocked gently, "leaving just means walking through a door into another room of my house. Of course, you would have had to redial my personal number, but that's no challenge for a bright, aggressive, corporate shark, is it?" She waited for a beat, then asked, "What can I do for you?"

"Tell me what's on your schedule for the weekend, starting bright and early tomorrow."

Brenna blinked, staring down at the telephone cord as if it had turned into a snake. It wasn't easy trying to beat Kane at his own game, she reflected wryly, mainly because she was never quite sure exactly what the game *was*. "Tomorrow?" she repeated cautiously. "Well...as a matter of fact," she said, taking a deep breath and throwing caution to the wind, "nothing." She had deliberately left the weekend open, knowing that one way or another she'd be spending the time with him. "I'm playing hooky."

"Good." There was a wealth of satisfaction in the word. "Come play with me."

Brenna absently studied the polished surface of her desk, absorbing the intimacy of his voice and the dual meaning of the invitation, wondering if they were deliberate, knowing without even thinking that they were. "Where?" she finally asked, determined not to commit herself without at least putting up a struggle. "And for how long?"

"Not too far. We'll cross the border and take a quick trip to Ensenada."

"How quick is quick?" she persevered. It sounded harmless, but she had learned that nothing was quite that simple with Kane Matthews.

"I don't know for sure. Maybe one day, maybe two."

Pulling her chair closer, she dropped into it and rested her head against the high back, contemplating the deliberately teasing quality of his answer. For a moment she considered telling him to head for one of the nearby beaches and take a long, wet walk; instead she moved the receiver away from her mouth and groaned. It wouldn't work, she decided. Kane didn't know the first thing about taking orders. She'd never get rid of him that easily. Besides, the whole purpose of this exasperating exercise was to be friendly and available—even if it killed her—until he wearied of the game. The only problem was that his stamina was proving to be greater than hers. She was already tired of the scheme and he showed no signs of flagging.

"Nope," she said, tucking the mouthpiece back between her chin and shoulder, "I'm not taking any overnight trips with you." There, she thought, breathing a sigh of relief. She couldn't make it any clearer. It was settled, over, finis.

"Why not?"

Clenching her teeth at the bland question, she pictured him sitting at his desk, taking a few minutes out of his busy schedule to see how high he could drive her blood pressure. He would be dressed in a dark suit, pale shirt and subtly striped tie, she decided. No, at this time of day the jacket was probably in his closet, his shirtsleeves would be rolled up to reveal strong forearms heavily dusted with dark hair, the button at his throat undone and his tie slightly loose; he would be the image of a man who had spent the day tearing the corporate world apart. More than likely he was leaning back, a slight smile turning up the corners of his firm mouth, waiting for her to come up with a handful of excuses, fully prepared to dismiss each one as soon as she voiced it.

No, she wouldn't give him the satisfaction, she decided as she rapidly sifted through her options. There had been very little discussion lately of the situation between them. Too little. Although she saw him every evening, she'd been spared any more visits with the accountant and realtor. It was tough living a life of duplicity, she decided with a martyred sigh, wondering how spies and double agents kept their lies straight. She was having a hard time simply remembering that she knew exactly why she was playing this ridiculous game and that he didn't! But while she might have doubts about some things, she was quite certain that she wasn't going to put herself in a situation where she'd have to spend the night with him, especially in a foreign country.

"I think what we have here," she said, rapidly improvising, "is a communication gap. And if you have to ask why I don't want to skip across the border for a couple of days, it's a big one."

"I'm listening."

Brenna took a deep breath, her mind a blank. Now that she had his attention, she hadn't the foggiest idea what to say. She certainly couldn't tell him that she was just playing for time, even though a man of his intelligence must be wondering why—if she really meant business—she hadn't severed the cord a long time ago.

"Kane," she began softly, "you don't know how I felt the morning after we, uh—" She coughed, suddenly aware of the deep pit she had just dug for herself.

"Loved each other until we were exhausted?" His voice was dry, and not very encouraging. "I have a fair idea."

Why couldn't he, just for once, say something that would help her? Brenna wondered, scowling down at the coiled telephone cord she was winding around her finger. "I don't think you do," she persevered. "I felt like I had been in bed with a stranger," she blurted, realizing that it was the truth. "You weren't the man I had known for six weeks."

"What about the one you've been with the past few days?" His deep voice was genuinely curious.

"He's an entirely different person," she wailed softly. "I don't know which one is you, or if *either* of the men I've met is the real Kane Matthews."

"What are you trying to tell me, Brenna?"

Good grief, how many ways did she have to say it? "That I need to understand you, to know you better," she said through clenched teeth.

"You want honesty? Warts and all? Everything out in the open?"

"Yes. It has to be that way before this . . ."

"Affair?" he asked blandly.

"—*situation* can go any further."

"And once you know me? Then what?"

"I don't know," she said honestly, forgetting that the entire conversation had started because she was trying to maneuver her way out of a tight corner. "Once we've reached that point, we can evaluate what we have and go on from there."

"I think you're right." His thoughtful tone surprised her.

"I know I am."

"But I have a condition of my own."

Brenna's brows drew together suspiciously. "What?"

"You have to give it a fair trial. You can't turn tail and run if you get mad. Or scared," he added softly.

"How much time do you consider fair?" she demanded, furious at the taunt, ignoring the fact that she had done exactly that just one short week ago.

"A month?"

"Sounds reasonable," she agreed rashly, indignation sweeping her along. It didn't move her too far, though. The same inner voice that had guided her successfully in the business world slowed her down. She clenched her teeth so that her impulsive tongue wouldn't get her in any deeper and tried to calm herself.

"Brenna?" His voice nudged her.

"Let's review the contract," she said briskly, pretending not to hear his single word of concern. "We get to know each other, right?"

"Right. I don't pressure you back into bed and you don't run the first time something in my charming personality bothers you. Right?"

"Right," she agreed, stifling a groan. Somehow she had the feeling that she had just complicated her future beyond anything she could imagine. But it wouldn't really be for a month, she consoled herself remembering the Plan. Kane was bound to give up before then.

"Can we get back to the Ensenada trip now?" Kane asked.

"One day," she said firmly, aware of the amusement in his voice. "That's the longest trip I'll take."

"Don't you trust me?"

Now there was a question! "Let's just say that I prefer to come home and sleep in my own bed, okay?" The word *alone* remained unspoken. "Besides, why Ensenada? Is there a reason, or did you just jab a pin in a map and come up with that particular city?"

"Have you ever heard of the annual Newport-Ensenada race?"

"Cars or runners?" she queried after a moment's thought.

"You haven't," he said with a sigh. "Do you know anything about boats?"

She didn't, and she didn't want to learn. The fact was that she turned a delicate shade of pea green if she so much as stepped foot on one, even if it was still tethered to a dock.

"You don't," he decided from her eloquent silence. "The race is for sailboats. It starts in the harbor at Newport and goes down to Ensenada, about a hundred and twenty-five miles in all."

Her stomach lurched at the very thought of such self-inflicted torture. "Kane," she interrupted firmly, "I'm the last person you should think of inviting aboard a boat. Believe me, I know what I'm talking about. I'm not a good sailor. Why don't we just pass on this one, okay?"

"I'm not trying to get you on a boat," he said in exasperation. "I want you to go down with me to meet one."

She tried to imagine the various reasons that drove people to the marinas and wharfs around the world to look at boats and couldn't come up with a solitary one. "Why?" she asked simply.

"Because a friend of mine is in the race and if the wind has been with him, he should get in to Ensenada sometime tomorrow. It's pretty wild at the finish and I thought you'd enjoy it."

That sounded harmless enough, she decided with relief. "You're sure I wouldn't have to get on the boat?" she demanded.

"Positive. Andy and his crew will be only too happy to get on dry land and find something cool to drink."

Brenna agreed to be ready early and slowly hung up. She picked up her briefcase and moved from the office into her living room. For once the cool combination of apricot and pale green failed to soothe her. The equally attractive ivory and blue of her bedroom was no more successful. She hung her navy suit in the closet and slipped into jeans and a T-shirt, grateful that she didn't have to face Kane for another twelve hours.

She padded barefoot into the kitchen, opened the refrigerator and wrinkled her nose at the dismal array of plastic-wrapped saucers and bowls. She had never figured out what drove her to save the remaining bits and pieces of meals. She hated leftovers and never ate them. But she conscientiously saved and sealed them, rotating them from the back of the shelves to the front. Only when they developed a peculiar odor or aquired a grayish-green cast was she able to toss them into the garbage disposal with a clear conscience. She examined the nearest ones, decided they still looked edible, plucked a shiny red apple from the crisper and closed the door.

If she could only be a bit more ruthless, she told herself for the hundredth time as she bit into the apple, her refrigerator shelves would be pristine. Her life would also be far less complicated. For one thing, she would have been able to say a resounding "no" to Kane Matthews that morning in her office; she wouldn't have allowed herself to be blackmailed into seeing him again. But no amount of ruthlessness, she admitted honestly to herself, would have made her walk away from him the night before that encounter. At that moment, nothing could have stopped her from responding to the darkly masculine force that eventually subdued her inhibitions and totally overwhelmed her.

She had to work on it, she decided catching a drop of tart juice with the tip of her tongue. She had to cultivate being hardhearted. Otherwise, she'd find herself in increasingly deeper and hotter water when dealing with Kane. The conversation she'd just had with him was a perfect example. On the surface nothing much had changed, but she had a sinking feeling that her strategy had received a definite setback. Before the call, her intention had been to make herself so available and compliant that he would be bored beyond measure and expeditiously remove himself from the scene. It was a simple plan, clearcut and definite. There had been no time line involved, as she'd explained to Julie, but it was obvious that it wouldn't take long for him to ease away. Now, somehow, at his prodding, she'd committed herself to what had all the earmarks of being a month's endurance test!

Twelve miles across town, Kane slowly cradled the receiver before hanging up. His soft laugh was a reflection of the anticipation gleaming deep within his smoky eyes. He hoped he was around to see the expression on her face when she realized the enormity of the commitment she'd just made. As he pulled a sheaf of printouts closer, a lingering grin still curled the corners of his mouth. She was made to be teased—as well as loved—and he couldn't resist doing either. He'd thought about making that call all afternoon. As far as that went, in one way or another, he spent most of his time thinking about her. And he couldn't remember a time when he'd looked forward to each new day as much as he had this last week.

The next morning when Brenna threw open the door in response to Kane's brisk knock, she knew the kid gloves were off. The way his eyes drifted over the fair hair framing her face, her snug yellow blouse, the curve of her hips beneath pleated white slacks, then stopped at her sandals and bare toes told her so.

He stood there, just taking her in. She hardly noticed; she was too intent on her own survey. In his blue knit shirt, brushed denims and new running shoes, he looked like someone touting the joys of a glamorous, high-priced resort. Except that he wasn't handsome enough to be a model, she thought as a touch of humor turned her eyes to jade. The carved planes of his face had nothing to do with mere conventional good looks. Unfortunately for her, she reflected anxiously, they had everything to do with pure animal magnetism.

Her fingers tightened on the edge of the door. His inspection was anything but cursory; he was taking his own sweet time and enjoying every leisurely second of it. Speculation and more than a tad of possessive approval were evident in his eyes. Brenna blinked at the taut challenge of the man before her and sighed. If this was what he meant by being open and honest, it was going to be a long day.

His gaze finally lifted and met hers. "Are you ready?"

"Good morning, Kane," she said politely, directing a cool little smile up at him. Simple courtesy, her grandmother had often told her, was a powerful bridge between cultures and warring factions. Brenna had recently discovered it was also great protective screening and it gave one a nice, satisfying feeling of being in control.

Kane stared down at her, a wry look in his gray eyes. "There's something about you that makes me forget the proprieties," he said finally. His small, wicked smile should have warned her. Actually it did—about a second too late. He bent down and deliberately brushed his lips across her mouth. They were hard and hungry. Raising his head and examining her stunned face, he murmured, "Now, have we forgotten anything else, or are you ready?"

She dropped her eyes to the strong line of his chin and muttered, "I'm ready." Snatching the lightweight jacket that matched her slacks and a colorful tote bag from the back of a nearby chair, she sailed past Kane, leaving him to lock the door.

As she dropped the tote on the back seat of his sleek car, the crackle of paper caught her attention, distracting her from a sudden onslaught of anxiety. Thinking of the notes dealing with Kane's interview that she had tucked inside her bag, she recognized the gesture for what it was: a foolish rationalization for spending the day with him. If his greeting was any indication of what the day would bring, it definitely didn't include business!

Fifteen minutes later she was still brooding over his tactics when they crossed the border into Mexico and swung west on Benito Juarez to link up with the freeway heading south to Ensenada.

"You know your interview is just ten days away," she reminded him in a worried voice. "You promised me three hours of uninterrupted time to work on it and so far we haven't even squeezed in fifteen minutes."

He reached out and cupped her knee with his hand. "I know. I'm sorry. This week has been a mess. How about late next week?"

"When we get back," she said, watching with fascination as his hand slid up and shaped itself to her thigh. "We've got to set a definite time. My calendar's almost full and, as good as I am, I can't seem to work in any more than twenty-four hours to a day."

"We'll do it."

"If we don't, I don't want you telling anyone that I helped you."

He grinned, flexing his fingers, seeming to take great pleasure in the feel of her. "In other words, if I bomb, I go down alone?"

"Right." She took his hand and put it back on the steering wheel. "You won't bomb without me," she said, looking up at his profile, "but with a few suggestions, you can dazzle them! And I've got a reputation to consider, you know." She was only half joking.

"Don't worry, I won't ruin it for you."

"I know you won't," she said evenly, "but I mean it. If you don't give me three hours, I wash my hands of the whole thing."

He glanced over at her, taking in her determined expression. She was a professional with a lot at stake, and he admired the stand she was taking. In her place, he'd do the same thing.

Even without her help, he wouldn't embarrass himself, Brenna thought, looking out over the sand to the frothy waves breaking on the beach. He had a good voice, an expert understanding of his subject and a natural ease that projected well on the screen. On almost any other show that would be enough for an adequate performance. But this was his first exposure to national TV, and he had to be better than adequate to cope with the controlled chaos of a studio and an ambushing host. Walton Kramer excelled at the hit-and-run style of interviewing. He had developed the skill to a fine art; his audience expected it and it kept his ratings high.

Still thinking of the slim, silver-haired host, she asked, "Have you had a chance to watch any of the tapes I gave you?"

"A couple." He stared at the straight road ahead. "Kramer can be a real bastard at times."

"Three hours," she reminded him with a grin. "That's all it will take to enable you to give him a dose of his own medicine."

He looked over at her. "How did you ever get started in this line of work?"

"You mean as a media consultant?" she asked, leaning back and savoring the genuine interest in his voice. During the past weeks they had each discussed the day-to-day running of their businesses but, she realized in surprise, they had never gotten around to this aspect of their lives.

He nodded. "That, as well as the etiquette business."

"We have to thank Julie's aunt and my grandmother for the initial training," she told him, noting with relief that he had temporarily switched off the sensuality that had been unnerving her. "Those two ladies came from completely different backgrounds, but they had one thing in common. They were both brought up by the book—the one written by Emily Post. When Aunt Deborah raised Julie, she taught her everything she knew. My grandmother did the same for me.

"Gram is a very nice lady and a real soft touch. Word got around, and she was always taking the wives of up-and-coming executives under her wing and helping them become successful hostesses. I can't even count the number of practice luncheons, teas and dinners she coached them through. I was almost always drafted as a guest, just to help fill up the table. Of course," she admitted with a chuckle, "I hated it. The last thing in the world I wanted to do was sit around a table with a bunch of women and mind my manners."

Kane grinned sympathetically. "When did you realize that you were sitting on a gold mine?"

"Years later. Julie and I both left the nest and somehow ended up as roommates at the university in Santa

Barbara. I was working on my M.B.A. and she was a communications major. Then, early in our last year there, I dragged her to a lecture I had to attend. We spent the evening listening to a corporate wheel complain that to-day's young business leaders were reared in the 'anything goes' atmosphere of the sixties and floundering in the world of finger bowls and crumbly French bread. He said that those who had a handle on etiquette moved ahead faster because they could relax over a meal and concen-trate on the conversation. It gave them a competitive edge. He also said that the higher up the ladder one went, the more social business became.''

"I see a flash of revelation coming," Kane drawled.

Brenna nodded, remembering the dawning excitement she and Julie had experienced. "You're right. We went back to our room and talked all night. Before daylight, we knew what we were going to do. Corporate heads are im-pressed by college degrees, so we finished school, got our pieces of paper and went into business."

"Did it work out the way you thought it would?"

"Um hmm. My education in business and Julie's in communication prepared us to run a business. And thanks to Gram and Aunt Deborah, both Julie and I have im-peccable style," she said with a grin, batting her lashes modestly.

"You're right about that, lady." He slanted a look down at her. "You do have style."

She drew in a sharp breath. "Anyway," she concluded hurriedly, staring at a string of run-down shacks at the side of the road. "Here we are."

"That covers the etiquette. What about the media training?"

Lulled by the even tone of his voice, she said thought-fully, "We slid into it sideways. One of our clients was slated to be on a forum on a local channel. We were able to help him."

"Another revelation?" he asked, smiling.

"A bolt of lightning," she agreed blithely. "We knew it would be a logical extension of what we were already doing, so we researched, studied and worked like the very devil to come up with a good training program."

"And what's ahead?"

"Bigger offices and more of the same. But we have to make some decisions pretty soon, because if we get much busier, we're going to have to expand the staff." Determinedly she changed the subject. "Your turn. How did the maverick get his start?"

He shrugged. "It's a dull story. I was always interested in computers. Once I knew more or less how they worked, I wanted to see what else they could do, so I started designing software."

Brenna waited. Finally realizing that no more was forthcoming, she said, "That's it?"

"I told you it was a dull story," he reminded her taking in her discontented expression.

"Short, too."

Kane sighed. "What else is there? I'm still involved in software."

A man of few words, Brenna thought—at least when it came to talking about himself. Terse. Succinct. Laconic, she added to herself, getting into the spirit of the thing. And concise. "I hope you manage to be a bit more vocal during the interview," she told him.

He looked over at her. "That's business, an entirely different matter. And it's not something we're going to worry about today."

Brenna stirred beneath the force of his smoky gaze. Open and honest, she remembered uneasily, that's what he

said he was going to be. She was just beginning to realize
what that promise meant. She had had one brief glimpse
of the real Kane Matthews—and had run from the reality
as fast as she could. Now she had a nasty feeling that she
was about to be reintroduced. Oh, he wouldn't try to rush
her back into bed. He'd said he wouldn't and she believed
him. Unfortunately their latest pact seemed to leave
everything else wide open!

Six

———

"This is Hussong's?"

"The one and only." Kane's hand slid down to her hip and tugged her against him, making room for a group of good-natured college kids who had turned from the bar and were looking for a place to sit. "What do you think?" He grinned at her baffled expression.

She looked around the room. The inside looked every bit as ancient as the weathered exterior. "Don't rush me."

"Want something to drink while you're deciding?"

Brenna nodded. "I'll grab that small table back there, while you get it. Beer for me," she said, recalling with a small shudder the day she had learned the hard way that outside the United States, the ice in mixed drinks could be just as lethal as impure water.

As she worked her way along the worn wooden floor, Brenna stared around the large room. It was undeniably a popular place, crowded with tourists and the first wave of

sunburned sailors from the race. Since practically half of
the cars in Southern California boasted one of the ubiq-
uitous "Hussong's Cantina" stickers on their bumpers,
and it was known as *the* place to be when in Ensenada, she
had demanded to see what made it unique. Now that she
was here, she wasn't quite sure what she had expected.
Perhaps a few strumming guitars and soft lights. Definitely not a time-worn structure that looked as though it
had survived as many storms inside as it had on the outside.

After winding her way through rows of miniscule
wooden tables and scarred chairs that quite possibly had
been there since the cantina opened, she stopped and stared
up at an enormous elk's head. Beside it, stretching all the
way to the rear of the room, was a solid wall of business
cards, held fast by straight pins, tacks and whatever means
had been at hand at the time. Brenna examined them
closely and found that they represented people from all
around the world. One enterprising Southern Californian
romance writer had left hers dangling from the elk's head.

She looked around when Kane set two cold bottles on a
small table. Joining him, she asked, "Do you think we'll
ever find your friends?"

He eased down into his chair with careless grace and
shrugged. "We may run into them, but if we don't it
doesn't matter. I didn't plan to spend the day with them."

"Oh." She blinked and said cautiously, "I thought that
was the whole purpose in coming down here."

"The whole purpose in coming down here," he said deliberately, leaning back and stretching out his legs, "was
to be with you."

"Oh." She lifted the bottle and took a long swallow. "I
just thought..."

"You thought wrong," he said gently.

"Oh." She stared at the bottle, touching it to the table several times, until she had formed a pattern of wet, interlocking rings. Looking up at Kane, she ignored his waiting expression and said brightly, "Well, it was a great idea. As much as I don't like boats, I have to admit that I'm glad I got to see even a part of the race. I suppose they'll still be coming in for hours."

"Um hmm."

"Those colorful sails are beautiful."

"The spinnakers?"

"Whatever. It was a breathtaking sight when each of the boats let them out for the last sweep into port."

"Um hmm."

"I didn't expect it to be anything like this," she persevered, running a slim finger through the wet rings. "People sitting in chairs on top of their RVs to watch the finish, flags flying—"

Reaching over to still her restless hand, Kane said, "When are you going to stop backing away from me, Brenna?"

Annoyed by the blunt interruption, she leaned back, taking her hand with her. "Did it ever occur to you that if you stopped pushing, I wouldn't have to?"

He placed his bottle on the table with angry precision. "Damn it, woman, I brought you down here to relax, not to drag you into bed. You said you wanted to get to know me better, and I can't think of a better time to start than right now. Can you?"

Green eyes slowly rose to meet gray ones and narrowed at the impatient challenge they encountered. Exactly how stupid did he think she was? He knew the effect he had on her. He couldn't help but know. Every time she saw that hungry look in his eyes, she made a fool of herself.

She thought longingly of those first, unthreatening weeks when she'd lived in a fool's paradise. She had discovered that they had a lot in common. They were both competitive, enjoyed the challenge of running their own businesses and they each had varied interests that overlapped at some points. Of course, she reluctantly admitted, that much was still true. At least that hadn't changed. Fine, she told herself wryly, if he's so wonderful, take him home with you, sign him up as a good friend.

There was only one problem with that. Every time she was fool enough to believe in such a simple solution, the image that had presented itself when she first compared Kane to other men returned in vivid detail. She pictured herself reaching out and, instead of touching one of those amiable spaniels, she found her hand resting on the head of a sleek, muscular Doberman, her eyes held by the waiting, unfathomable darkness of his. No, there was definitely no way that she and Kane could settle for something as simple as friendship.

It was too bad, she thought with genuine regret, because friendship with Kane would be like having solid bars of gold stashed away in the bank. She had the feeling that his loyalty was as unfaltering as his honesty. He was strong, smart and...undeniably male, she finished wryly. A possessive male, at that. One who would take over a relationship and turn a peace-loving woman's life upside down. And that, she decided as she shifted restlessly, was the problem in a nutshell. She couldn't handle a man like that. What he needed was another type of woman. One who enjoyed a challenge.

She sighed wistfully, allowing herself a couple of seconds to dream. But she wasn't that woman. It was as simple as that. Although, for some incomprehensible reason, he thought she was. She considered that intriguing idea briefly. He saw her as sensual, sexy. Female to his male. It was a heady thought. Especially for a woman who had spent little time contemplating that aspect of her life.

She slanted an uncertain glance up at him—and almost choked at the hungry expression in his eyes. If she was smart, she told herself, she'd get up and walk out of this place without a backward glance. But she wasn't. She'd obviously lost every shred of intelligence she possessed the day she met Kane. And to complicate matters, Brenna realized with a start, sometime during the past two months she'd become addicted to playing with fire! She obviously had a death wish; that was the only possible explanation. Otherwise she wouldn't be sitting across a tiny table from a man who exhibited all the earmarks of a predator getting ready for the kill!

Kane lifted his bottle to his lips and swallowed the last of the beer. Someday he'd learn to keep his mouth shut and to take what was being offered, he told himself disgustedly. He hoped it didn't happen too late. He was tired of having Brenna look at him as if she expected to have a chunk bitten out of her luscious body. Actually, he thought whimsically, all he wanted to do right now was nibble a bit. His eyes licked over her, touching here and there, mapping his course. He'd start right at the soft spot where her throat and shoulder met, he decided, then he'd slide down the curve of her breast to—

"I've decided," Brenna said abruptly, derailing his train of thought, "that I like this place. It has ambiance." She gave the word its French pronunciation, slurring it dramatically.

Kane thoughtfully considered his empty bottle as well as his options. He could keep her on the topic at hand and make the afternoon miserable for both of them or let her change the subject and salvage what he could. His eyes rested on her face for a moment.

"What kind of ambiance?" he asked in resignation, his decision already made. He'd take whatever she was willing to give. If a smile was all she was going to offer, he'd settle for that now and get the rest later.

"It's perfect for a tequila western," she said with relish. "Can't you just see the bad guy, dressed all in black, coming in through the swinging doors—"

"There aren't any swinging doors."

She dismissed the trifling objection with a wave of her hand. "He stands in the doorway, checking out the long bar, looking for the hero—"

"Who just happens to be wearing a white hat?" Kane encouraged.

"Of course. The good guys always wear white. Maybe a bit smudged, but definitely white."

"And what is *he* doing?"

"Sitting in the corner having a drink," she said promptly. "Trying to peel a hot-eyed senorita in a ruffled skirt off his lap."

Kane surged to his feet, wrapping his fingers around Brenna's wrist and muttering an oath beneath his breath. That did it! Her lighthearted scenario was fine up to the hot-eyed part. At that point his body had taken over, responding to the image he'd substituted of Brenna wrapping herself around him. Now, he either had to move or resign himself to using the table for cover.

"Come on." He tugged at her hand, bringing her along in his wake as he headed for the door. "We haven't even scratched the surface of this town."

An hour later, Kane looked down at her. "Are you all right?" he asked, eyeing her flushed face narrowly.

"Sure. Fine." Brenna touched her forehead cautiously. "A little hot, but fine," she assured him.

"I should have my head examined, keeping you out in the sun like this." He took her arm and hustled her past a street vendor, who was pushing a white cart and lustily advertising his fish cocktails. She tried to slow him down so that she could take another look at the plastic cups filled with shrimp and crab. It had been a long time since breakfast. Kane didn't break his stride and, sighing philosophically, she kept up with him.

"Where are we going?" Brenna asked, edging around a man with a flashing gold tooth who grinned invitingly and held out a foam rubber alligator on a stick. The sidewalks were like one long, continuous flea market, lined from corner to corner with vendors selling cheap jewelry, serapes, luggage, belts and buckles. The idea seemed to be that whatever the crazy gringos would buy, they would sell.

"I want to get you a hat." Kane stopped and looked around.

"I don't need one."

He pointed across the street. "We'll go over there."

Brenna dug her heels in. "I said I don't need a hat. Just get me in the shade for a while."

Kane led her over to what appeared to be an animated stack of sombreros. When they worked through the crowd of bargaining tourists, Brenna saw that it was actually a slim young man with about twenty hats balanced on his head.

After stopping the youth, Kane turned to her. "Pick one," he ordered succinctly.

On the verge of telling him what he could do with sombreros in general and these in particular, she took one look at the young man's imploring smile and caved in. "I will if you will," she told Kane.

He nodded and said something in rapid Spanish to the boy. His words galvanized the young man into action. He flipped the hats down on a piece of cardboard and sifted through them, pulling out one for Brenna and urging her to try it on. It was straw with a yellow band that almost matched her blouse. He even withdrew a speckled mirror from his vest pocket and held it so that she could see her reflection.

It fit, she noted with surprise. The young man obviously knew his business. Brenna curled the side brims up and tilted the hat forward, aware that Kane was quietly going about the job of finding one for himself. She gave a final tug at the brim and smiled at the boy. "I'll take it. Did you find one?" she asked, turning to Kane. He had moved a few feet away to another stack.

"I can't decide," he said over his shoulder, motioning her to his side. "Come here and help me."

Curious, and with a faint smile curving her lips, Brenna stepped closer. Kane wasn't the type who needed to have his opinions confirmed. If she had thought about it at all, she would have expected him to know exactly what he wanted and to buy it with a minimum of fuss. Instead he was standing patiently by some beautifully made hats that were either genuine Stetsons or fantastic clones. When she looked down at his final selection, her smile faded. In one hand he held a glistening white hat, in the other, a jet-black one.

"What do you think, honey?"

Brenna's gaze moved slowly from the hats to his face, which was as blandly innocent as his voice. The faint gleam of amusement in his eyes was the final straw—or it would have been if she hadn't also seen a fleeting look of hopeful expectancy. She lowered her head, the straw brim of her hat shielding her face. At least she hoped it hid the exasperation she was battling. He was pushing again. Of course, according to him, he didn't push.

The hell he didn't!

Brenna stared at the two hats until Kane shifted restlessly. It would serve him right if she took the black one and pulled it down around his ears. The only thing that saved him was the fact that beneath all that pushy machismo, he was as vulnerable as anyone else. At least she was going to give him the benefit of the doubt and assume that he was. It didn't really matter, she decided in disgust. Her heart was obviously as soft as her head. She couldn't deliberately hurt anyone—even Kane when he was driving her to distraction.

But that didn't mean she was going to make it easy for him. She let the silence stretch out. When Kane cleared his throat, she looked up and held out her hand for the white hat. His sudden smile faded when she pointed to the remaining one and said, "Why don't you try it on?"

Watching him jerk it down over his brow, she said conversationally, "You just never know how things are going to look until you try them. Is it the right size?"

"It fits fine," he said, biting off the words.

Frowning thoughtfully, Brenna said, "I don't know. It seems kind of stark, maybe you ought to try this one."

Watching her with narrowed eyes, Kane switched hats, some of the tension leaving his shoulders.

"Hmm." Brenna tilted her head and stared up at him, refusing to acknowledge that he looked magnificent in both of them. Finally she shook her head. "It's not you," she stated profoundly. "Don't they have something in between? Maybe in gray, to match your eyes."

Kane's lips twitched. "How about this?" he asked smoothly, reaching for a soft pearl gray hat.

He was tugging at the brim when Brenna said sweetly, "I was thinking more along the lines of charcoal."

Before she knew what was happening, Kane wrapped his arms around her, lifted her up, and held her tight against him. She could feel his soft crack of laughter vibrating through her whole body. "Okay, I deserved just what I got," he admitted several seconds later when he lowered her to the ground. "But we've still got a problem. Which one do I take?"

Brenna heaved a sigh. The man simply never gave up! "It's a tough decision," she complained. "I suggest we compromise." She led him back to the straw hats and handed him one.

Later, while the youthful entrepreneur was digging for change, Kane muttered, "I still want an answer."

"Don't push, Matthews," she warned, looking up and nudging her hat to the back of her head. "I may never figure it out."

He took her hand and led her away. "You will," he assured her with a confident smile that rattled her. "Soon." He changed the subject abruptly. "Are you hungry?"

"Starved. I'm just about ready to chase down that little man with the fish cocktails."

"Forget it. The last thing you need is a flaming case of turista."

"That'll never happen," she declared, eyeing the little white cart longingly as Kane hauled her along with him. "I traveled a lot with Gram. I cut my teeth on every bug known to man."

Over lunch, Brenna entertained Kane with stories of her travels. She still managed to consume her share, he noted with amusement. She sampled everything on the table, enthusiastically dipping into hot salsa loaded with enough jalapeños to strip wallpaper.

"My mother is a sad lady," she said in answer to his question. Pointing to the salsa, she asked, "Don't you want some of this?" He shook his head and she said, "Where was I?"

"Your mother is sad."

She nodded, finished a taco with dispatch and smiled at the waiter who took her empty margarita glass and replaced it with a full one. "She isn't, her situation is."

Kane quietly waved away a second waiter who was heading in their direction, never taking his eyes off her.

"My mother is a chameleon," she told him earnestly. "She's fallen in love—" her fingers made quotation marks around the word "—more times that I can count. Each time she took off with the man and tried to become a clone. If he was an artist, she tried to paint. She studied landscaping when she was with the gardener. She doesn't have the foggiest idea what it's like to be happy with herself. She doesn't even know who she is. I made a promise to myself a long time ago that I'd never be like that." She dipped the last tortilla chip in the salsa and nibbled on it, washing it down with the last of her margarita. After wiping her mouth and checking her blouse for spots, she placed her napkin on the table.

"Sure you didn't miss anything?" Kane grinned at her blissful sigh, wondering if she knew just how much she had told him.

"Don't pick on me." She surveyed the ravaged table with contentment. "I don't get to pig out on stuff like this very often. I'm too busy taking culturally deprived executives to regular restaurants and leading them through the intricacies of multiple forks and artichokes. As much as I love it, I never recommend eating food like this at a business lunch. It's too messy."

Kane signaled the waiter and ordered another round of margaritas. Turning back to Brenna, he asked, "Do you really get enough work to keep you busy?"

"You've been helping me look for a larger office," she reminded him, amused by his half-disbelieving frown. "Business, as they say, is booming. What are your parents like?" she demanded suddenly. "Where did they come from?"

"A small town in the midwest."

"What did your father do?"

"He owned a clothing store."

"Ah hah!"

He groaned. "What does that mean?"

She waited while a salt-rimmed glass was slid in front of her. "It means that you just told me everything I need to know about your upbringing and why you can't believe that anyone actually needs my services." She took a swallow from the glass and closed her eyes, savoring the tart, lime-flavored drink.

"First of all, your parents were hardworking people in a financial bracket somewhere slightly above middle class. From the time you were old enough to sit in a regular chair at the table, manners were drilled into you. By the time you were ten or eleven, your parents could invite the mayor for dinner and you could eat whatever food they served without embarrassing them. How am I doing so far?"

Kane nodded, his intrigued gaze never leaving her face. "Go on."

Lifting her shoulders in a slight shrug, she said, "There's not much more to say. Your family probably moved out here when you were in your teens. You have no trace of a midwestern drawl or accent," she explained kindly, responding to his raised eyebrows. "Your father probably also went into business for himself out here. You met his

Silhouette's
Best Ever "Get Acquainted" Offer

Look what we'd give to hear from you

6 FREE GIFTS 6

Return This Sticker
and Get 6 Gifts—FREE
Compliments of Silhouette

**GET ALL YOU ARE
ENTITLED TO—AFFIX STICKER
TO RETURN CARD—MAIL TODAY**

This is our most fabulous offer ever...
AND THERE'S STILL ➠ MORE INSIDE.
Let's get acquainted.
Let's become friends—

Look what we've got for you:

5 FREE GIFTS

...A FREE bracelet watch
...plus a sampler set of 4 terrific
Silhouette Desire®novels,
specially selected by our editors.

FREE MYSTERY GIFT

...PLUS a surprise mystery gift
that will delight you.

All this just for trying our Reader Service!

If you wish to continue in the Reader Service,
you'll get 6 new Silhouette Desire®novels every
month—before they're available in stores.
That's SNEAK PREVIEWS with 10% off the
cover price on any books you keep (just $2.24★
each)—and FREE home delivery besides!

Plus There's More!

With your monthly book shipments, you'll also get our newsletter, packed
with news of your favorite authors and upcoming books—FREE! And as
a valued reader, we'll be sending you additional free gifts from time to
time—as a token of our appreciation for being a home subscriber.

THERE IS NO CATCH. You're not required to buy a single book, ever. You
may cancel Reader Service privileges anytime, if you want. All you have
to do is write "cancel" on your statement or simply return your shipment of books to us at our cost. The free gifts are yours anyway. It's a
super sweet deal if ever there was one. Try us and see!

★Terms and prices subject to change without notice.

Get 4 FREE full-length Silhouette Desire® novels.

Plus
this lovely
bracelet
watch

Plus
a surprise
free gift

▼ PLUS LOTS MORE! MAIL THIS CARD TODAY ▼

Silhouette's Best-Ever "Get Acquainted" Offer

Yes, I'll try Silhouette Books under the terms outlined on the opposite page. Send me 4 free Silhouette Desire® novels, a free bracelet watch and a free mystery gift.

225 CIS JAYW

PLACE STICKER
FOR 6 FREE GIFTS
HERE

NAME _____

ADDRESS _____ APT. _____

CITY _____

STATE _____ ZIP CODE _____

Offer limited to one per household and not valid to current Silhouette Desire Subscribers. All orders subject to approval.

PRINTED IN U.S.A.

Don't forget...

...Return this card today and receive 4 free books, free bracelet watch and free mystery gift.

...You will receive books before they're available in stores and at a discount off the cover prices.

...No obligation to buy. You can cancel at any time by writing "cancel" on your statement or returning a shipment to us at our cost.

If offer card is missing, write to: Silhouette Books
901 Fuhrmann Blvd., P.O. Box 1867, Buffalo, N.Y. 14269-1867

associates, sometimes at home, sometimes in restaurants. Right?"

He nodded again. "That still doesn't explain—"

"Wait!" She raised her hand, palm facing him. "Let me finish. Whether you know it or not, you were groomed perfectly for what you're doing. Your manners are so deeply ingrained that you don't even think about them. You can attend a banquet or meet a customer at an exclusive restaurant, order a meal without thinking twice about it and talk while automatically selecting the proper utensils. I bet you never worry about what to do with your napkin or which side your bread plate is on, do you?"

"Of course not," he began, "but—"

"My clients do," she interrupted. "They worry constantly about everything. Do you know why? Because most of them were reared in the 'anything goes' atmosphere of the sixties with a lot of people who had different ideas about what the important things in life were. Others come from low-income families and if they ever went out to dinner it was to a small neighborhood restaurant that served plain and hearty food.

"I've never had a client who was ill-mannered or inconsiderate. Most of them are instinctively courteous. They've simply never been taught the little things that make such a big difference."

Kane took a swallow of his drink, absorbing the passion that shimmered in her eyes, turning them to emerald. He longed for a mirror to set in front of her so she could see herself for the small, ardent creature that she was—so she could glory in the revelation. Or would she run from it this time, too? he wondered, his mind taking him back to the memory of flushed cheeks, of eyes stunned and glistening with runaway emotion. That night she had touched him with shy, curious hands, fingers that caressed and kneaded, arms and legs that wrapped around him, holding him captive even as she surrendered body and soul.

His body tightened and he swore softly. It was taking all the self-control he possessed—and some he didn't even know he had—to back off and give her the time she needed. And she thought he was pushing her? Hell, she didn't even know the meaning of the word. When he decided to push, there'd be no doubt in her mind or anyone else's!

Brenna placed her glass back on the table and licked salt from her lips. "Sorry," she said briefly, hooking an errant strand of hair behind her ear and looking anywhere except at Kane. "You touched an exposed nerve."

"Tell me the rest," Kane said, his voice as soothing as a caress. "I know how you feel about your clients, now tell me how you feel after a seminar."

Her lips curved in a smile that put dreams in her eyes. "Like a magician," she said softly. "They pay hard cash for information, and they get their money's worth. After it's over, I answer every one of their questions. Much of the time I'm simply affirming what they know intuitively. But the thing that satisfies me the most is the bonus that I give them."

"Bonus?" Kane was so busy telling himself that Brenna would someday give him with that same dreamy gaze that he barely knew what he was saying.

"Um hmm." Her eyes met his. "They come for specific information, and they leave with self-confidence. Once they have that, there's no stopping them."

Kane touched the back of her hand with a gentle finger. "You're a real hotshot, aren't you?"

Brenna finished her margarita with a flourish and thumped her glass on the table. "Yep," she said complacently. "That's exactly what I am."

A couple of hours later, they strolled back to the port. Brenna had haggled gleefully over a velour sweat suit and a long robe made of crinkly material. Kane carried the spoils.

They wandered around until they found a spot in the shade where they had a good view of the incoming boats. Kane leaned against a post and wrapped his arms around Brenna, tugging her into the cradle of his body. She relaxed, muscle by muscle, until the curve of her bottom snuggled against his thighs and her back pressed against his chest.

"Too bad we never found your friends."

"Umm."

"Is that a yes rumble or a no?"

"It's a God-this-feels-so-good-I-never-want-to-move rumble." His hand slid down from her waist and possessively spread over her stomach, holding her in place.

He was right, Brenna reflected, sinking deeper into him. It did feel good. Without moving her head from the hollow of his shoulder, she gazed around at the boats. There were hundreds of them bucking against the ropes that held them captive at the docks, and almost as many bobbing and weaving in the water. Swallowing, she followed their movements—the never-ending motion of more boats than she had ever seen in her life. She swallowed again, with great determination.

Kane took his eyes off the scene before him, tightening his arms around Brenna before he realized that she was trying to unwrap his hands and move away. Her whole body was pulled tight as a bowstring, resisting his touch.

"Brenna?" He bent his head until his lips touched her ear. "Honey, what's the matter?"

Her voice was tightly controlled. "Let me go."

"Tell me what's wrong," he demanded, moving his hands to her rigid shoulders.

"Kane," she gasped, "I'm going to be sick!"

Seven

There's a spot on the wall."

Kane glanced up from his magazine at the first sound of Brenna's husky whisper. He didn't have far to look. At some point during the endless night, he had pulled a worn plaid chair next to the bed so she could see him when she opened her eyes.

"So there is," he agreed calmly, touching her forehead with his palm. At least the spot didn't move, he thought. The weekend of the big race was no time to stay overnight in Ensenada without reservations, and he had taken the first thing he could find. The motel was run-down, definitely not five-star. It barely deserved one. The room was small and dark, but it had a bathroom and a bed and there was nothing crawling on the walls, so he could live with a spotty paint job.

Brenna looked around, taking in the dingy curtains at the single window and the threadbare carpet. "Where are we?" Her voice sounded appallingly weak to his critical ear.

Reaching out to take her limp hand in his, he grinned. "Honey, this is what every man fantasizes about. I have a gorgeous blonde in a seedy motel across the border and God only knows what's in store for me."

"You're sick, Matthews," she muttered wanly, sliding her thumb over his fingers. "Sick."

"Not me." He moved over and sat on the mattress, his hip touching hers. "You're the patient. At least for now."

Brenna shivered and closed her eyes. "What time is it?"

"Almost dawn," Kane told her, covering her shoulders with a soft blanket.

"Have you been here all the time?" she asked sleepily.

"Just about." Except for the time he'd paid the owner's wife to stay with Brenna while he rushed out to several stores. He'd returned loaded down with new sheets and a blanket, cleaning supplies, a variety of over-the-counter drugs and some bottled water and soft drinks. "I went out and found my friends, and we hit a few bars."

That opened her eyes. She stared up at him for a long moment. "Funny," she murmured, not believing a word of it. "Must have been boring, sitting here all night."

"Yeah." Of course, scrubbing down the bathroom and taking her in there about a dozen times had livened things up a little. While Kane watched, her eyes closed and she took a deep, shuddering breath. He thought she had dozed off again, but she blinked and lifted her heavy lids.

"I'm not seasick," she informed him.

He smiled at the cranky statement. "I never thought you were."

"I only get seasick when I'm *on* a boat."

"That sound reasonable. Do you think you can handle some 7-Up?"

Brenna frowned, giving the matter a great deal of thought. "I don't know," she finally said.

"Do you want to try? I'd like to get some liquids in you."

Nodding cautiously, she said, "Just a little."

When he returned with a small glass and slid his arm behind her to raise her up, she stared at him with too-bright eyes. Apparently under the impression that she had failed to convince him, she said, "When I'm *not* on a boat, I never get seasick."

Holding the glass to her lips, he ordered gently, "Drink." He waited until the tumbler was empty, then slowly lowered her to the pillow. He braced his hands on the mattress, one on either side of her shoulders, and looked down at her for a long, searching moment. "I believe you," he finally said in a gentle voice. "You never get seasick unless you're out on the water."

"That's right," she murmured.

"I will never, ever, take you on a boat," he promised, brushing her hair away from her face.

"Good." A moment later she was asleep.

Kane looked down at her with a fierce frown, wondering if he should have given her that brown syrup the druggist had recommended. God only knew what was in it. The label on the back of the bottle promised it would cure everything from heartburn to hangnails, but he was fast losing confidence in the stuff. Brenna's trips to the bathroom were just as frequent as they had been earlier, and the racking spasms had not diminished.

He paced restlessly between the door and the bed, running his hand nervously through his hair. She had obviously picked up a local bug. He should have taken her to a hospital. The thought had nagged him all night, intensifying every time he carried her into the bathroom and supported her shivering body against his. It would have been the sensible thing to do. He could still do it. Every bit of logic within him told him that he *should* do it.

The only problem was, he couldn't. His decision was based more on his own gut feeling than the fact that he was in another country. Kane rarely went to a doctor, but when he did, it was to one who had come highly recommended and had been investigated thoroughly. He would do no less for Brenna. She'd have to be a lot sicker than she was now before he'd put her in the hands of a possible incompetent.

Coming to a stop at the side of the bed, he looked down at her, reflecting that he was being both illogical and unreasonable, if not downright crazy. He couldn't think of anyone less qualified to handle the situation than the person who was in charge right now. He didn't know a damn thing about dealing with illness, but he had followed his instincts for too many years to ignore them now. And right now he was *feeling* illogical and unreasonable.

Kane popped open a soft drink and sat back down in the chair, the decision made. If push came to shove, he'd bundle her into the car and head for home. He estimated that the usual ninety-minute drive could be done in about an hour.

"Oh!" Brenna sat up with familiar urgency and threw back the covers. Her face was white and strained. "Oh, damn!" she wailed softly. Her feet touched the floor just as Kane scooped her up and headed for the bathroom. They had the whole wretched business down to a system by now, and within just a few minutes she had used some of the bottled water to brush her teeth and was tucked back into bed.

The next time Brenna opened her eyes, rays of late afternoon sun were working their way through the dingy curtains. With a lack of curiosity that would have amazed her at any other time, she examined what could be seen of the room without moving her head. A rickety table beside the bed held two small glasses and a spotted brass lamp. A six-pack of soft drinks sat on a scuffed dresser, and the chair that Kane had used was empty.

She had barely registered his absence before she discovered that she knew precisely where he was; the warmth pressing against her backside informed her. If that hadn't done it, the heavy arm circling her waist and holding her possessively in the crescent of his body would have. Or the large hand that cupped her lace-covered breast.

Lace. Part of her mind contemplated the significance of the unfamiliar flimsy covering while another part pieced together the events that had led to the two of them sharing the small bed. She didn't remember much after the first bout of nausea, beyond the fact that Kane had hustled her to a nearby rest room and called to the women inside that he was coming in with her—and that he'd handled the nasty interval with considerable aplomb. She vaguely recalled that several of the women had been charmed by him, handing him damp towels and clearly willing to be of additional service.

After that, there were a lot of hazy spots and even more blanks. What little she did remember wasn't pleasant. "Seasick," she muttered in disgust. Apparently she had reached the point where she couldn't even stand around and watch the water.

"Mexican flu," Kane told her pleasantly, giving her breast a gentle squeeze. She shivered, at both his touch and at the light abrasion of lace against her sensitive flesh.

Tucking a languid hand beneath the blanket and running it along the material—bypassing the muscular arm encircling her waist—she discovered that her nightgown was lacy on top and silky from the point beneath her breasts to the bottom. Since the skirt ended just below her hips, there wasn't much silk to speak of. Of course, there wasn't a heck of a lot of lace, either. She sighed. It was just the sort of thing a man would buy for a dying woman.

When she finally realized what Kane had said, she gathered her pitiful remnants of energy and said, "You're wrong." She hoped she wouldn't have to argue the matter. "I never pick up local bugs."

"Turista," he said blandly.

To someone in Brenna's fragile condition, he not only sounded disgustingly healthy, but as though he was prepared to discuss the matter at great length. Slowly she looked over her shoulder at him with narrowed eyes. His expression gradually lightened, a gleam of amusement softening his assessing gaze. She glared at him and said very distinctly, "No."

"Yes." With his chuckle rumbling along her back, he added, "And the way you were guzzling that salsa, you're lucky you don't have a hole in your stomach."

"You're supposed to treat sick people with sympathy," she told him grumpily, exhausting herself in the process.

"I did that all night long, but you've slept for a solid six hours, so I figure I can pick on you."

Annoyed, she said, "I want to turn on my back." There was clearly no use arguing with the man, so she waited while he reluctantly released her, making a big production of running his hand over her thigh and straightening the skirt of whatever it was she was wearing. Finally he gave her about three inches of space and helped her roll over.

"Why didn't you take me home?" Her throat was raw and her voice not much more than a croak, but her expression made it clear that this time she wasn't being difficult, merely requesting information.

"You needed instant access to a bathroom."

His blunt answer satisfied her. He was right. If memory served her correctly, she wouldn't have gotten two blocks before trouble set in. "What do we do now?"

"I don't know." He closed his eyes. "I figure that with your penchant for being in control, in another five minutes or so you'll be slinging orders right and left."

Blinking furiously at the weak tears that filled her eyes, Brenna stared up at the cracked ceiling. He was right, she thought wearily. She fought him tooth and nail whenever he crowded her. She was independent and self-sufficient. Usually. And she would be that way again—tomorrow or the next day. Strong, capable and very determined. But right now she felt as though someone had bored a hole in her and hollowed her out. She was as weak as a newborn baby and, although she'd crawl home on nails and tacks before she'd admit it, she yearned to be spoiled a little. To be coddled and taken care of and gently bullied. She didn't want to be in charge of anything.

"Hey, what's this?" A gentle finger traced the silvery trail from the corner of her eye to her hairline. "Brenna? Babe? Look at me." It was an order, gently spoken, but an order nonetheless.

She ignored it. Instead she squeezed her eyes shut and tried to contain the hot tears that were steadily dripping down her temple.

The bed shifted as Kane rose to his elbow. "Honey?" He touched the trail of tears and swore softly. He carefully turned her toward him and wrapped her in the warmth of his arms. "I'm an idiot and I should be shot." He snuggled her closer. "I was teasing," he murmured, his lips touching her ear. "I wanted to give you a few minutes before I got you up."

Brenna dampened his bare shoulder. "I can't even turn over by myself," she wept.

Kane soothed her with long strokes of his hands and whispered things like, "There, there" and "That's all right," which made no sense at all but eventually dried her tears.

"I can't get up," she complained fretfully when she realized what he wanted her to do.

"How does your stomach feel?"

"Sore."

"But settled?"

"I guess so."

He kissed her on the tip of her nose. "Then it's time to move on to bigger things. Stay where you are." He tucked her back on the pillow and rolled out of bed. Moving around to her side, he said, "I'm going to put you in the chair and see if you can sit up for a while without getting sick."

Brenna's eyes roamed over him, listlessly taking in his naked body.

Kane's mouth curved slightly. "Don't worry, I'll get some clothes on in a minute. Right now, I want to get you up." He pulled back the blanket and said, "Relax and let me supply the muscle. If this works, I'll put you in the car and we'll head for home."

Brenna woke up and plucked at the cocoon of blanket that Kane had kept wrapped around her when he'd tucked her into the car. "This is ridiculous." Her voice was stronger and not so whiny, she noted gratefully. She had fallen asleep the moment he had put the key into the ignition, and she felt noticeably better.

"Leave that alone," he ordered, reaching out a hand and tucking a corner behind her shoulder. "We're almost at the border and you don't have a hell of a lot on underneath it."

"I noticed," she murmured dryly.

"Ah, feeling better, are we?" He slanted a glance over at her and smiled. Looking ahead, he said, "We're sliding in just before the Sunday night traffic jam. Things are looking up."

Within fifteen minutes they were on the outskirts of San Diego. "You need to take the next turnoff to get to my house," Brenna reminded him.

He gave her a look that told her to forget it. "We're going to my place."

Brenna bristled, forgetting all about her earlier desire to be coddled and spoiled. He had an infuriating way of snapping out orders, she decided.

The silent revolt, brief as it was, tired her. The flash of adrenaline faded, leaving her weak and weepy. She contented herself with a watery glare.

A short time later, Kane pulled into his garage and woke Brenna from a light doze. Going around to her side of the car, he opened the door, tucked the blanket around her and lifted her into his arms. With a minimum of fuss, he had her into the house and settled on his bed.

Brenna looked around the familiar room, and even in her weakened state it brought back too many memories. "I'm not—"

"You are," he said flatly. "You just may need me tonight." Leaving her to ponder the nuances implicit in the statement, he rummaged through a drawer and tossed a couple of T-shirts on the bed. Brenna closed her eyes and listened to the rustling noises he made as he moved around the room.

"Do you think you can handle some food?"

A low rumble from her stomach answered him before she could.

"I guess that's a yes."

She looked up and met his small smile with one of her own. "I'm famished," she told him in surprise.

"Good. We'll start off with something light."

He was a handy man to have around, Brenna mused a few minutes later. She was still wrapped in the blanket, sitting in the chair where he had placed her, watching him move around the kitchen. Not that fixing tea and toast required a lot of expertise, it was simply the way he had handled the last twenty-four hours. There was something to be said for a man who saw what needed to be done and did it without a fuss, she admitted grudgingly.

She nodded her thanks when he placed a cup and small plate of toast in front of her. Nibbling on the crisp bread, she watched as he turned away to make himself a sandwich. But then it was never his competence that she'd questioned, Brenna reminded herself wearily. The thing that rattled her the most was the way he just assumed that he was always the one in charge. It was a quality that tended to annoy other people who pictured themselves the same way. She took a swallow of tea and looked questioningly at Kane. He was lounging against the sink, eating.

He shook his head. "I'll stay here. It's no fun watching someone else eat when your stomach's upset."

She sighed. He was right, of course. Again. Brenna knew she was being unfair. And petty. And ungrateful. She was also a bit overwhelmed. How on earth was she going to keep him at a distance after this? Setting the cup carefully on the table, she shook her head. She needed more vitality than she presently had to cope with that one.

After Kane took her empty dishes to the sink, he turned, resting his hands on his hips. He looked down at her, watching her wilt as waves of fatigue washed over her. "What'll it be," he asked softly, "bed, or a shower?"

Brenna had a sudden, overwhelming need to feel hot water streaming over her body, torrents of it cascading down and removing the ache deep within her bones. But when she tried to stand and found that her knees wouldn't work, she had sudden doubts. With each passing moment, though, the lure of soap and water grew stronger. She'd cope. Somehow. She didn't care if she had to sit on the tiled floor and let the water pour over her, *nothing* was going to stop her.

"A shower," she said, hoping she sounded more energetic than she felt.

A narrowed-eyed look brushed over her, then Kane slowly nodded. Without a word, he picked her up, carried her into the bathroom and perched her on the edge of the tub. "Don't move a muscle," he ordered. He disappeared into the bedroom and was back before she had a chance even to think about disobeying him. He dumped some clothes on top of the hamper and turned back to peel the blanket from her.

Even with the door closed to shut out drafts, she was cold. No wonder, she decided, staring down in disbelief at the skimpy pink thing that covered bits and pieces of her. "What *is* this?"

Kane couldn't contain his grin. "I think they said it was a nightgown. A short one," he clarified.

"It certainly is," she agreed faintly, turning an accusing look on him.

His shrug informed her that he wasn't going to waste a lot of time discussing the matter. "I made a quick run out to several stores. You needed something to sleep in. I told them to pick out a gown in your size and wrap it up."

Amusement crept back into his eyes. "Imagine my surprise when I opened it."

For the first time in twenty-four hours, Brenna had color in her cheeks. "Who—?"

"I did," he said flatly. "I put you into it, and I'm taking you out of it." Brenna blinked as his hands moved to her shoulders. Before she had decided that it wasn't worth arguing about, the concoction of lace and silk was in a pink pool at her feet. He led her to the enclosed shower, opened the door, turned on the tap, adjusted the temperature and gently stuffed her in, closing the door behind her.

Brenna shuddered under the impact of the water, grimly considering the possibility that she just might end up sitting on the tiled floor, after all, when the door swung open again and Kane stepped in behind her.

She turned and spread her hand on the creamy tiles, staring at him. The stinging spray was bringing her back to life, she decided with a slow blink. He was beautiful, made as a man should be made: wide shoulders, narrow hips and long, muscular legs. Dark hair sprinkled his body in a pattern that her hands had once hungrily traced. "What are you doing here?" she whispered.

He looked down at her, his mouth set in a straight line. "You're too weak to stay in here long, so let's get moving," he ordered briskly. "Hold on to my shoulders." He worked up a lather in his hands and smoothed it over her breasts, back and hips in long, gliding strokes, stopping to massage the tight muscles around her neck.

There was nothing sensual about the way he did it, Brenna lectured herself as he bent down and repeated the process from her thighs to her feet. In fact, he acted as though he couldn't get it over fast enough. She turned obediently when he moved her away from the water, splaying her hand on the cool tile wall where he put it, supporting herself while he quickly soaped himself down.

Kane rinsed the frothy lather from his body and reached out for her again. With one hand lightly gripping her waist, he adjusted the flow of water and urged her into the gentle stream.

"Oh! It's getting cold," she gasped, turning in the circle of Kane's arm, her back to the spray. She slipped then clutched his shoulders and fought to regain her balance.

"You're okay, I've got you. No problem." Kane's arm tightened, hauling her against his solid body.

No problem? she wondered. Maybe. She could be forgiven for having a few doubts, she decided, since she was being pressed back against the hardness of a fully aroused male.

Eight

Fatigue and weakness didn't exactly stimulate one to clever repartee, Brenna reflected in silent disgust, so she did the only thing she was capable of: she stayed precisely where she was, not moving a muscle.

Slowly, by infinitesimal degrees, Kane's arms loosened around her.

Despite her condition, she realized that the control he demonstrated by releasing her merely served to heighten the tension between them. Hurriedly searching for some light comment to break the silence, she lifted her hands from his shoulders and stepped back as far as his grasp would allow.

It wasn't far enough. The hardening tips of her breasts brushed against the curling hair on his chest. When she took a quick breath of protest, it brought her just that much closer.

Slowly, reluctantly, Brenna lifted her head, her eyes trailing up from his shoulders and finally meeting his. Wry exasperation gleamed in his gray gaze, along with a stark hunger that he couldn't quite conceal.

"I'm sorry," she said simply. "I wasn't teasing."

Kane nodded abruptly. "I know, honey." He lifted one shoulder in an eloquent shrug. "What we have here is a very minor problem, but it's *my* problem. Besides," he said with a sudden grin, "we have an agreement, remember? Everything is out in the open now. No pretending."

Raising his hands to frame her face, he said, "You concentrate on getting well, and I'll take care of my...fractious body. Come on, let's get out of here."

Brenna slowly released the breath she had been holding and turned, stumbling as she stepped through the shower door. The electric episode, brief as it had been, had obliterated whatever strength she'd gained from the small meal. Kane's arm around her waist was all that kept her on her feet.

Fatigue was no longer gently washing over her. It was now a tidal wave, rushing in to wrap her in its powerful embrace, sucking her out to dizzying depths then dropping her, allowing her to sink deeper and deeper into—

"Brenna!"

Opening her heavy eyes at the sharp command, she looked into the steamy mirror and met Kane's worried eyes. "I'm okay," she muttered, so weary that she could hardly move her lips.

"Two minutes," he promised, grabbing a heavy towel and running it over her in brisk, no-nonsense strokes. When she was dry enough to satisfy him, he ordered, "Put up your arms." She obeyed, blinking when he dropped one of his cotton T-shirts over her head. Then he propped her on the edge of the tub and towel-dried her hair.

"I have to go...to work tomorrow." She mumbled the words as Kane carried her to the bed. Her head rested securely on his shoulder, her arms twined around his neck.

"I called Julie. She said not to worry, she'll cover for you." The rumble of his voice vibrated against the side of her breast.

"You've been very...patient," she muttered sleepily, sighing with pleasure when he slid her between the sheets. "Very nice."

"Tell me that again when you're well," he said in an amused voice.

"Mmm." Brenna threaded her fingers through his and promptly fell asleep.

This could be a dangerous habit, Brenna reflected sleepily the next morning before she even opened her eyes. She knew exactly where she was—in Kane's bed. More specifically, lying on her side with her head in the hollow of his shoulder. A loose T-shirt was bunched around her waist and one of her legs rested cozily between his. A large hand curled possessively around her breast.

From the even rate of his breathing, she decided that Kane was still asleep. That gave her at least several minutes, she calculated, focusing her eyes thoughtfully on the mat of curling dark hair that covered most of his chest. She was going to need every second. Detaching herself and sliding out of bed without disturbing him was not going to be an easy task.

But there was no doubt in Brenna's mind that her life would remain much less complicated if she could do exactly that. It was one thing for Kane to handle and sleep with a near-nude body that was also near-dead. It was an entirely different matter for him to wake up and find a healthy, if starved, seminaked woman plastered to him.

Debating the merit of first removing her leg or his hand brought her no nearer to a decision. It was a toss-up, she reflected philosophically. Either way he was going to wake up, so she might as well get at it. Holding her breath, she cautiously slid her leg from between his and snaked her hips back an inch or so. Just as she was congratulating herself on a successful maneuver, Kane's hand dropped to her bottom, shaped itself to the curve of her hip and tightened. Before she realized his intention, he scooped her up and moved her on top of him.

"What are you doing?" Brenna scowled down from her perch, balancing herself by grabbing his shoulders.

He smiled up at her, a sleepy, dangerous smile, and kept his hands on her bare bottom, holding her in place. "Good morning."

Brenna narrowed her eyes. "Kane," she warned, "this isn't funny."

He seemed to consider the matter. "You've lost weight," he said after tracing her rib cage with an idle finger.

She closed her eyes in exasperation. When she opened them, a shiver worked its way down her spine. His gaze was pure seduction. He wanted her. He didn't try to hide it. It was all there in his eyes—a wordless, potent challenge. Determination mingled with the familiar gleam of hunger. And patience. He would have her, he told her in silent warning. When the time was right, he would take her and the chase would be over. And when it was, she wouldn't make a fuss, because she would come to him willingly.

Then suddenly it was gone. The silent threat, the battle of wills. What was left, though, was almost as troublesome: a dark-haired pirate with a morning stubble and a bland expression. Brenna blinked warily.

"Are you hungry?" One hand slid down to test the resilient flesh of her thigh.

"I'm starved, and I'm also tired of this game. Let me go." Her frown deepened when he finally released her. He lifted his shoulders in a slight shrug and raised his brows, mutely implying that whatever her problem was, he had no part in it.

Brenna made a maddened sound deep in her throat and slid off him, managing to dig an elbow in his ribs when she moved. "You're really cute, Matthews," she muttered, pulling down the T-shirt and scooting to the edge of the bed.

"So is your...birthmark," he said politely, looking straight at her bottom, which was barely covered by his shirt.

Scowling, she stalked over to the bathroom, telling herself she wouldn't slam the door. When his soft laugh followed her, she forgot all about her good intentions.

A few minutes later, she slowly opened the door and peeked out, looking for something to wear besides Kane's shirt. Noting with relief that he was no longer lying in the rumpled, massive bed, she padded into the masculine room and discovered that sometime during the evening he had brought in their packages. She poked around until she found the velour sweat suit and trotted back into the bathroom.

By the time she climbed the stairs to the kitchen, the aroma of coffee was drifting down to meet her. "Ah, just where I like to see the man of the house," she declared brightly, hoisting herself onto a stool and propping her elbows on the bar. "In the kitchen carrying his weight. And so efficient that there's nothing left for me to do but sit."

Kane's gaze lifted from the scrambled eggs to the provocative expression in her eyes. "You can slide your sweet butt off that bar stool and pour some juice into those glasses," he directed, a swift grin lighting his face as he pointed at the tumblers on the counter. He liked having Brenna in his kitchen. As far as that went, he liked her in his shower, in his bed, lying on the floor by the fireplace and in every other room in the house.

There wasn't much about her that didn't please him, he decided, except her stubborn determination to kick him out of her life. Once they got that little matter straightened out, they would be able to get on to the more important things—like when she would move in with him.

"Your eggs are better than the ones I make," she told him a few minutes later as she greedily scooped up another forkful.

"How can you mess up scrambled eggs?"

"Let me count the ways," she mumbled. "My grandmother gave up on me a long time ago. Believe me—" she shook her head dolefully "—it's a hopeless cause. I can set a beautiful table and eat anything on it with style and grace—I'm quoting Gram, in case you're wondering—but I can't cook worth a darn."

"It doesn't seem to worry you."

She shook her head cheerfully before she took another swallow of coffee. "Nope, it doesn't. I have a job that requires me to eat about half of my meals in some of the best restaurants in town at someone else's expense. The rest of the time I pop frozen dinners into the microwave."

"Is that in the nature of a warning?" he asked calmly, crunching down on a piece of toast.

"Warning?" She blinked at him, her green gaze curious. "Did I miss something?"

He shook his head. "I was just wondering if you'd thought of a new way to try to discourage me."

She watched him impale the last piece of sausage with his fork and pop it into his mouth. "New way?" she repeated cautiously, not planning to get near enough the rest of his comment to touch it.

Kane wiped his mouth and crumpled the paper napkin. Leaning back, he said evenly, "Do you honestly think I don't know what you're up to?"

She gave innocence her best shot. "Are you so sure I'm up to something?"

"Yes."

"I didn't know I was so obvious."

"You try not to be, but your hopeful expression gives you away. Why don't I just simplify things with a little honesty?" he offered, gazing at her averted face. "I'm not going to lose interest, and I'm not going to walk away from you."

Brenna stiffened, looking down at her coffee mug. Was she really that transparent? she wondered ruefully. Probably. Looking back over her life, she remembered that she had never been successful at telling lies, white or any other variety.

"If you recall," he continued, eyeing her narrowly, "I told you the morning after we made love—"

"Slept together."

"Made love." His voice was as hard as the expression on his face. "I told you that what we had was something special, and there's no way in hell that either of us can pretend it didn't happen. Do you remember?"

Brenna nodded slowly. "Yes."

"Tell me something, honey."

Lulled by his soft voice, she looked up. "What?"

"Did you really think of it as a one-night stand?"

Brenna flinched at the question. It was as relentlessly direct as his gaze. "Damn it!" she sputtered, "how can you ask me a question like that?"

"It's easy."

"You know how I feel," she said stiffly, sudden heat crawling up over her breasts and settling in her face.

"If I did, I wouldn't ask. Whenever I've said anything about making love, you've corrected me with cool little statements about sleeping together or going to bed. If that's all it meant to you, we're in trouble, honey." Silence filled the cheerful room, then he said softly, "Will you tell me? Please?"

Brenna would have preferred to argue the matter. As a matter of fact, she fully intended to, but she made the mistake of turning her head and looking right into his eyes. What she saw there stopped the hasty words she was about to utter.

For one fleeting second, his expression was a complicated blend of dread, hope, expectancy and a few other emotions she couldn't name. She blinked at the naked vulnerability she saw in his face. It was gone so quickly, replaced by a veiled look that tried for nonchalance that she wondered for a moment if she had been mistaken. Unfortunately she knew she hadn't.

How on earth could she shore up her defenses with a flippant comment if he offered her vulnerability and honesty, and expected it in return? It wasn't fair, she fumed silently. Besides, how did you put something like that into words? Her experience with intimacy was very limited. In fact, she reflected, realizing with a shock the abject poverty of her experience, she had never *talked* about making love with anyone.

Brenna's primary reaction to the insight was one of awkwardness. She was intelligent, well-read and far above the age of consent, for heaven's sake. Yet she knew that if she tried to tell him what she had experienced that night, she would blush and stammer like a schoolgirl. Besides, telling him would be the equivalent to jumping from the frying pan into the fire. There was no way on God's green earth that she would be able to keep him at arm's length after that.

"Brenna?"

The drawled question interrupted the nagging little internal voice that was busily telling her she *owed* him the truth. At this point she wasn't sure if it was right or wrong, but apparently she wasn't going to be given the time to find out. Kane was definitely applying pressure.

Stiffening her spine, Brenna stared directly at the top button of Kane's shirt. "You saw how I reacted," she said in a distant voice.

"Yeah, I sure did."

"Well?" Belligerence warmed the word a bit. "You're a businessman. Can't you reach a logical conclusion from the evidence of your own senses?"

"I did."

"Good," she said briskly. "End of discussion." She poured some coffee into her mug, checked his, saw that it was full and replaced the pot.

"Not quite," he told her.

"Why *not*?"

"Because the conclusion I reached was that you were as wild as I was, that what happened to you was as incredible as what happened to me."

"Do I hear a 'but' in there?" she inquired stiffly.

Kane's narrowed eyes examined her flushed cheeks. "Damn right you do. But I wonder if I'm wrong every time you say you *slept* with me. You weren't sleeping then, damn it! Sleeping is what you did last night."

Casting an irritated glance at the ceiling, Brenna decided that she was either crazy or blind. Kane Matthews was about as vulnerable as an armored truck! But he had his teeth well and truly into the subject and he wasn't about to let go. Oh, hell, she reflected moodily, this wasn't getting either of them anywhere. Apparently there was only one way to end the whole, painful subject.

Gritting her teeth, Brenna took the plunge. "You were right," she admitted with all the joy of someone about to have a tooth extracted.

"About what?" Kane raised his brows and waited.

"Your, uh, original conclusion," she tap-danced.

"Which one was that?" he asked obtusely.

Brenna gritted her teeth. "About me being a wild woman. I wanted you. All over me, in me. And I couldn't keep my hands off you," she ended in a rush. "Now," she demanded brusquely, getting up from the table, "are you satisfied?"

Kane's hand closed around her wrist before she left her chair. "No."

Brenna sat back down with a thump. "What do you want? *Blood*?"

He shook his head. "I want you to talk to me without turning scarlet or trying to run. But most of all, I want to know how you felt."

Shooting him a black glance, Brenna said, "I just told you."

"I want a feeling, Brenna." His hand still shackled her wrist and he gave her a slight shake. "Not what you wanted or what you did. An honest-to-God feeling."

Brenna opened her mouth and nothing came out.

Kane waited, then said softly, "How did you feel when we made love, honey?"

Not "slept," she noted. Not "went to bed." Made love. The man was as unyielding as a wall of granite.

"Honey, I need the words more than I've ever needed anything in my life." The truth of his statement was etched on his face. "I *need* to know. I thought it was as good for you as it was for me, but now..." He broke off and shrugged. "Tell me how you felt when you got hot and damp at my touch, when I moved inside you, when—"

"Stunned," she admitted in a whisper, stopping his words by putting her fingers on his lips. "Excited, fulfilled for the first time in my life. I didn't know it could be like that. I was hungry, so hungry, and you fed me with your body. I felt weak and you gave me strength. I ached with emptiness and you filled me. I was awkward and you made me believe in my own beauty. I thought we would be so... *earnest*, and you taught me the joy of teasing, of laughter."

Her gaze locked with his, kept there by the dawning wonder in his eyes. "I had begun to wonder what all the fuss was about," she admitted with a wry smile. "You showed me. It was—" she lifted her shoulders in a slight shrug as if searching for words "—glorious. For the first time in my life I understood what it meant to be a woman."

Kane drew in a sharp breath and closed his eyes for several long moments. When he opened them, he said, "My God, woman, when you finally open up, you go all the way, don't you?" Brenna blinked at the smile transforming his face.

I *knew* it, she thought wrathfully, almost dizzy from the wicked flash of white teeth against tanned skin. The vulnerable man might never have existed. In his place was a modern day, victorious gladiator, a buccaneer gloating over his booty!

Tugging her hand from his grasp, Brenna jumped to her feet. "Don't get any bright ideas," she snapped, taking her dishes over to the sink and scraping them energetically. "This doesn't change a thing. You may be hell on wheels in bed, but you're a whole bunch of trouble that I just don't need."

Kane placed his plate on the sink. "I know."

"You're the type of man who walks in the door and takes over."

"I know."

Brenna turned on the water more forcefully than she'd intended. "And I don't like to be taken over."

"I know," he soothed, nudging his mug closer to her.

Turning in exasperation, she demanded, "*What* do you know?"

He wrapped his arms around her and hugged her, grinning down at her frustrated face. "That you're running as fast as your gorgeous legs will carry you."

"You're right," she agreed sweetly, slipping out of his grasp and turning back to the sink. "And I'll keep on running until you admit that I'm right." She wiped the counter and dried her hands on the towel. "But right now, the only place I want to run is home. Can you take me or do you have to get to work?"

Kane draped his arm over her shoulder and aimed her toward the door. "I'm going in for a while. Get your things."

Later that afternoon, Brenna reached for the telephone. "A Touch of Class, Brenna MacKay speaking. Oh, hi, Larry. You sound nervous, is tomorrow the big day?"

She leaned back and propped her stockinged feet on the desk, crossing them at the ankles. Lawrence Manley, an up-and-coming tiger in the corporate jungle, had been in their last seminar. His business savvy couldn't be faulted, but he was falling apart at the thought of hosting a cocktail party.

Listening to his litany of insecurities, Brenna shifted in the chair until she was comfortable. "What hors d'oeuvres are you serving?" she asked as soon as he stopped for air. "Sounds wonderful," she commented after a moment, "especially the stuffed mushrooms, Larry," she soothed, breaking into another stream of gloomy predictions, "it'll be a great success. You've done all the ground work, now all you have to do is relax and enjoy yourself."

She moved the receiver away from her ear as the volume increased. "The people will talk to each other, I promise you. Think of it this way, you're giving them a great opportunity to do some networking." She smiled at the sudden, thoughtful silence. "The most difficult thing you'll have to do is remember to hold your drink in your left hand so your right one isn't cold and clammy when you shake hands."

She laughed softly at his wry response. "I *know* you can handle it. Oh, if you really want to wow them, tip the valets ahead of time for the entire party. You can't imagine how impressed your guests will be when they don't have to stand in the parking lot and dig around for a couple of bucks."

A slight smile lingered on her face. "It's been my pleasure, Larry. After it's over, call and tell me what a success it was." She replaced the receiver and looked up.

"Was that Larry Manley?" Julie asked.

"Um hmm. With bridal jitters."

"He'll do fine."

"That's what I told him," Brenna said, getting up and heading for the door.

Julie's scrutiny was thorough. She examined Brenna's face, then checked her from top to bottom as she followed her through the office into the living room. "You lived through Mexican flu, I see."

Brenna wrinkled her nose. "I still can't believe it. Turista!" she said disgustedly.

"Kane sounded rattled when he called. How bad was it?"

Motioning for Julie to take a chair, Brenna dropped down on the sofa and stretched out with a deep sigh. "Bad enough." She shuddered at a particularly noxious memory. "I don't know what I would have done without him."

Julie slipped off her shoes and tucked her legs beneath her. "Okay, now that I know you're better, talk. I want all the gory details."

"Starting when Kane hustled me into the women's rest room and held my head over the basin?"

"Really?" Julie grinned and settled deeper into the chair. "The man has guts, I'll give him that."

"Walk, do not run, to the end of the line. All the other women thought so, too."

"Poor baby. Did he get all the attention?"

Brenna gave a dramatic sigh. "It was disgusting. They were all over him, like ants at a picnic. They told him he was wonderful."

"And so he was. Did you tell him that you thought so, too?"

"I was . . . busy. Do you want to hear the part where he got me to a seedy motel and took off my clothes?"

"Ah, I know if I waited long enough we'd get to the X-rated stuff."

"Or," Brenna's voice softened, "how he scrubbed down the bathroom and bought new pillows, sheets and blankets for the bed."

"Brenna, that's positively romantic." Julie flung out her arm and declaimed, "These moldy sheets aren't fit to touch my lady's silken skin!"

"I felt the same way," she admitted. "I almost cried. I felt . . . cherished, I guess." She stared up at the ceiling, remembering when she *had* wept and how he'd taken her into his arms.

Julie sighed. "How else was Mr. Wonderful wonderful?"

"He bought me a nightgown to keep me warm." Brenna ruined the prim statement with a wicked sideways glance.

"Black and slinky, I hope."

"Pink. Silk and lace."

"Ah."

"About ten square inches of each."

"Aha!"

"He *said* that he didn't pick it out, that he just told the salesgirl to find one and wrap it up."

"I believe that, don't you?"

"Certainly."

Their laughter was a soft sound in the comfortable room.

"Actually," Brenna admitted, "I *do* believe it."

"Why?"

"Because of the expression on his face when he told me about unwrapping it."

"Something to do with poetic justice?"

Brenna chuckled. "More along the lines of a good deed being its own reward."

"So," Julie said, breaking the thoughtful silence, "the shark came in handy, did he?"

Brenna nodded. "He knows how to get things done."

Looking at her friend's expressive face, Julie said, "May I assume that Plan A is alive and well?"

"Well..."

"Already?"

"He knew exactly what I was doing," Brenna said disgustedly.

"So much for a secret plan. Now what?"

"I, uh, sort of got talked into another one."

Julie groaned. "I assume that it's Kane's plan?"

Brenna looked at her friend thoughtfully. "More of a combined effort," she said finally.

"It's sounding worse all the time." Julie uncurled her legs and stood up. "Hold everything until I get us some iced tea." When she returned with two tinkling glasses, she said, "Go ahead. I can't stand the suspense. I want it all, right down to the fine print."

Somehow, Brenna thought as she explained the new arrangement, it didn't make as much sense as it had when she'd discussed it with Kane. Or perhaps Julie's stunned expression was affecting her judgment.

"Everything out in the open?" Julie repeated.

Brenna nodded, her mind leaping back to the scene in the shower. Kane certainly hadn't been hiding anything then!

"Warts and all?" Julie croaked.

Brenna's nod was slower this time.

"And you signed up for a month? Girl, where did I go wrong with you?"

Sitting up, Brenna said earnestly, "No. This arrangement really does have some merit. I *do* need to spend more time with Kane when he isn't pretending to be someone that he isn't."

Julie's fascinated stare followed her when she moved to the end of the couch. "Why?"

"I want to see if he's really as high-handed as I thought he was," Brenna said simply. "We both know that I couldn't live with a man who might expect to take over and run my life. But if I'm wrong, he has definite possibilities! Besides, there's something he needs to learn about me."

"I'm going to hate myself for asking," Julie said. "But I'll bite. What?"

Brenna stroked a velvet throw pillow absently, then gazed at her friend. "Kane has some very...inaccurate ideas about the kind of woman I am. He thinks I'm sensual and..."

"*What*, for heaven's sake!"

"Sexy. Wild. And hot."

Julie regarded her with utter fascination. "And of course you've got to show him that you're none of those things."

Brenna firmly pushed away memories that centered around Kane's fireplace. "Exactly."

Setting her glass on a nearby table, Julie said, "I think I want to join Kane's team."

Nine

"Marcie, you're going to be fine, honest."

Brenna beamed confidence into her voice and aimed it through the telephone. Marcie Minters, young and a little rough around the edges, was taking her first important client to lunch at a fancy restaurant. For ten minutes she had wavered between the conviction that she wouldn't survive the ordeal and knowing that she would commit some unspeakably gauche act and not *deserve* to survive.

"What are you going to order for lunch?" Brenna asked, attempting to channel Marcie's nervous energy into positive action. "Do you have a copy of the menu? Good. Start looking. Remember, you want food you don't have to fuss with so you can concentrate on your client and his business."

A small sound in the doorway distracted Brenna, and she looked up with a quick frown. Kane stood there, a lean shark in a dark blue suit, looking ready to gobble up the

other fish in his pond, regardless of size or weight. His pale
blue shirt made him look tanner than ever and deepened
the gray of his eyes. At the sight of him lounging there with
his own brand of casual grace, a look of lazy appreciation
in his silvery eyes, Brenna sucked in her breath. And
promptly choked.

"What?" She coughed and moved the earpiece closer,
waving Kane to the chair beside her desk. "No, Marcie,
avoid soup. Especially French onion. You'll get long
strings of cheese on your spoon that will stretch out for
three feet."

She shook her head, her gaze following Kane as he am-
bled over to look out the window. "No pasta that you have
to slurp, no sandwiches that will fall apart in your hands."

Having Kane in the room where she couldn't see him
made Brenna restless, so she stood up and paced the length
of her desk. He kept moving, slowly examining framed
pictures and certificates. She turned slightly to keep him in
view and came to a dead stop when he looked directly at
her, raised questioning brows and half smiled.

"Do you remember any of the things we suggested at the
seminar?" she said rapidly, turning her back on him and
concentrating on Marcie.

Kane's hand tangled in the silvery-gold hair brushing
against Brenna's shoulders. Lifting the silky strands, he
bent his head and sniffed delicately, absorbing the light
floral fragrance that belonged to only one woman in the
world, then dropped a soft kiss on the exposed, tender
nape. "Umm." It was a husky growl of satisfaction, a
sensual invitation. Slowly he traced a series of delicate
kisses down her neck to the edge of her scoop-necked
blouse.

Brenna shivered. "Quiche?" she repeated breathlessly.
"Good choice. How about some fresh fruit to go with it?

And a muffin. That'll keep you away from crusty bread that scatters crumbs all over the table. It will look nice, and you can relax over the meal and concentrate on the conversation." She sped through a few more suggestions, sighing when relieved noises came through the receiver.

When Kane gently ran a finger along the path his lips had just blazed, she shivered again. "It was my pleasure, Marcie," she said, turning and slanting a black look at him. "Wrap up that contract in a big, red ribbon and call us back. We love success stories."

She cradled the receiver and frowned up at his teasing grin. "I'm going to have to take you in hand," she said in a severe voice.

"Good." He leaned back against the desk, his eyes inviting her to smile. "When?"

"When one executive visits the office of another, there is such a thing as appropriate behavior," she scolded. "Do you do things like this very often?"

"Almost never." He released her hair, watching it fall around her shoulders in a swirl. "I'm usually pretty well trained. It's just that I find San Diego's maven of propriety irresistible."

Removing herself to a safer distance, Brenna dropped back in her chair. "I'll get even, you know."

"God, I hope so!" His deep chuckle matched the amusement gleaming in his eyes. Taking the chair next to hers and pointing to the phone, he said, "I thought you told me you gave these people confidence. Whoever that was slept through part of the seminar."

Brenna shrugged. "Last minute nerves. It happens to a lot of them. We consider it part of our job to hold their hands through the first big event. After that—" she waved a hand airily "—they leave the nest and fly."

Looking at him through narrowed eyes, she changed the subject abruptly. "I hope you brought your appointment book. We've *got* to schedule some work time, and it has to be soon."

With all the flair of a magician pulling flowers out of his sleeve, Kane produced a leather volume from the inside pocket of his jacket and held it up for her inspection. "Here it is, just as you ordered," he murmured, deliberately provoking her.

Her cool green eyes swept over as much of him as she could see, settling for a moment on the crisp cuffs of his shirt, then on the backs of his large, capable hands, dusted with a sprinkling of dark hair. Strong hands, she remembered. Tender hands, clever hands. Blinking, she brought her mind back to the subject under discussion.

"You know," she said conversationally, "I've always had a pleasant disposition. I like working with people and they like me. But in two months, you've turned me into a nag and a shrew."

"Only with me, honey," he assured her. "And I enjoy having you try to whip me into shape."

"You annoy the hell out of me, and when you're not doing that, you drive me nuts. I don't know why I bother with you."

"You're wild for my body."

Brenna chuckled, her eyes laughing up at him. She was seeing another side of Kane, one that he'd tamped down along with his aggressiveness for those six weeks. He was clever and entertaining—witty without ever crossing the border of good taste. I *like* him, she thought, startled by the realization. And dismayed. She could argue with a man who meant nothing but trouble and chaos, push him out of her life, even if she *was* wild for his body. But it was much harder to fight a man you liked, she admitted with a silent groan.

Kane touched her on the shoulder near the rolled sleeve of her green dress. "Nice," he approved. "I've never seen you wear anything like this in the office."

Nodding, Brenna said, "There was no need to haul out the business suit today. I don't have any classes so I'm concentrating on paperwork. You, on the other hand, look ready to go out and chew up the competition." She reached out and touched the fine wool fabric of his suit. "By the way, this is the perfect outfit to wear for the interview."

"That's what I thought. I decided that you'd feel better if you got an advance glimpse of it."

"You wore it just to show me? I'm flattered."

"That was one reason. I'm also taking a buyer out to lunch. Want to come along and see that I use the right fork?"

"You'll do fine," she said dryly, opening her large desk calendar. "What day? Thursday? Friday? Three hours before the interview on Monday?"

Kane quelled a grin and slid a hand beneath her silky fall of hair, curved it around her nape and gently squeezed. He knew he'd be tarred and feathered by the worldwide sisterhood if he admitted it, but he wanted to throw her over his shoulder and carry her off to bed when she tried to slug it out with him. She was half his weight and got a crick in her neck when she looked up at him, he reflected, running his assessing gaze over her. Still, she never backed off.

He admired that. He was also damnably aroused by it. Of course, he thought ruefully, he was in a constant state of half arousal around her. It played merry hell with his body and didn't do a thing for his disposition.

Brenna tapped her pencil on the desk. "Come on," she prodded. "let's make a big executive decision here."

"Friday." Kane slid his hand away, touching her ear-lobe with the tip of one finger, then settling back in his chair. "How about three?"

She shivered at the light caress and tried to hide the fact by reaching for a pen. "I don't believe it," she muttered, jotting his name down in the book. "A day *and* a time. I must be living right."

Kane blocked out a three-hour period and returned the leather-bound volume to his pocket.

"Be sure to tell your secretary about that so she can put it on the master calendar," Brenna instructed briskly, closing her book and putting it aside.

"You really *are* bossy, aren't you?" Kane looked down at her, lazily enjoying the flicker of doubt that crossed her face. He enjoyed even more the slight shrug that told him she was going to keep right on pushing.

"It's good for you," she assured him. "Without me, you'd keep putting things off and make a mess of the whole interview."

Brenna was aware of the predatory expression in his eye. Lately she had become adept at spotting that particular look. Mainly because it was around so often, she reflected, avoiding his gaze. Kane tended to look on the month moratorium as a license to hunt, and she was getting tired of feeling like the prey.

"You really think I'd blow it?"

"No," she said honestly. "I told you before, you could do a good job without me. You only need me if you want to be terrific!"

Kane unbuttoned his jacket and leaned back, returning her teasing glance. "Patting yourself on the back?"

"A little," she admitted, smiling. "Just reminding you how good I am."

"I haven't forgotten." He stood up and went over to the window. Leaning against the sill, he said, "Actually I came early so we could talk for a while, to see if there was anything you wanted me to think about until we get together on Friday."

Brenna narrowed her eyes in thought. "If I knew more about your business, I could help anticipate the types of questions he might ask you. What on earth have we talked about for the past couple of months?" she asked in surprise. "All I really know is that you design software and own your own company. What do you *do* when you design software? What are you working on now?"

Hoping that he would respond in words of one syllable, Brenna lamented that it was too late to take a crash course in computers. Or to conceal the extent of her ignorance. In this day and age it was almost a sin against motherhood, country and apple pie to be computer illiterate, most definitely. Julie had offered to take charge of the office PC, mainly because she was afraid Brenna would erase all the disks as she fumbled through a simple operation.

She watched Kane slide his hands into his pockets, the gesture pushing his open jacket back behind his wrists. He stared thoughtfully at the brown carpet, and she stared at him. He was a picture of masculine grace, long strong lines and rough angles. And he was beautiful. Stunned by the sudden thought, Brenna turned her head and deliberately studied the one modern painting she had on the wall. Unfortunately its clean, sensual lines reminded her of Kane.

"I'm working on something to ferret out and destroy viruses," he said slowly.

Brenna brightened. A medical program. She was no brain surgeon, but she knew more about flu bugs than PCs and software. "How did you get involved in that?" she asked, picturing him in a white lab coat surrounded by glass vials. "Isn't it a little out of your territory?"

He looked up, surprised. "Not really. We have a lot of government contracts."

"What branch of the government?"

"This one is for the military."

"What do they plan to do with it?"

"In a sense, 'inoculate' themselves."

Frowning, Brenna asked, "You mean at places like veterans' hospitals?"

"No."

"They want it for the troops?"

Kane stared at her. "What troops?"

"*Any* of them. You know, soldiers, sailors and marines?"

"Honey, what the hell are we talking about?" He moved away from the window and propped himself against the corner of Brenna's desk. He noted gratefully that she looked as confused as he felt.

"Your work," she said promptly. "At least I thought we were. You mentioned a virus and I thought about sick people." She sighed in resignation. "I think it's turning out to be more complicated than I thought. Who gets sick?"

Kane chuckled. "*What* gets sick. It's a computer virus that infects programs. And I'm trying to develop an antibody."

"Tell me this is a bad dream," Brenna begged. "Something out of a science fiction movie." She looked at him with narrowed eyes and said, "You're kidding."

He just stared at her.

She sighed. "You're serious."

He nodded, the corners of his mouth curving. "Maybe you'd better tell me how much you understand about computers."

She held up her hand and brought her finger and thumb together, leaving enough space to accommodate a sheet of tissue paper. "About that much."

"I was afraid of that." He stared thoughtfully down at the tips of his shoes. "In a nutshell, here's how it works. The virus is spread via computer bulletin boards, data bases, or shared floppy disks."

He paused and Brenna nodded automatically. She didn't have the foggiest idea what he was taking about.

"Sometimes it's planted by a prankster, a hacker showing off. They'll send a message along with it."

"Message," she repeated numbly.

"Yeah, they'll say something cute like, 'Hi, I'm a virus. Try to find me.' Then troubleshooters are called in to find it before any damage is done. Sometimes they're lucky."

"*What* damage?" Brenna heard her voice rise a couple of notches. She stopped, cleared her throat and repeated, "What damage?"

"It destroys the program."

"And that's bad."

His nod was grim. "In one country, it destroyed the network of a leading financial system. In Europe, they're battling one that causes malfunctions on all Fridays and the thirteenth of each month. On Friday the thirteenth, the virus erases the computer's entire storage system."

"Good grief, it's *worse* than a science fiction plot. What can you do?"

"Keep looking for a better mousetrap. Each time one is found, a new virus crops up and another fix is needed."

Brenna looked at him with respect that bordered on awe. "And that's what you do?"

His sudden grin was a flash of white against his tan. "Finally. You're impressed. If I'd known that's what it took, I'd have wowed you weeks ago."

She got up and threaded her fingers through his leading him through the office and into the living room. "I am indeed," she assured him. "I am also going to be totally useless when it comes to anticipating questions from your friend and mine, Walton Kramer." She waved him to a seat on the couch and perched on the cushion next to him.

Turning to face him, she said, "But I can show you some of the tactics he'll use."

"That's good enough. I should be able to take it from there." Kane reclaimed her hand and rested his head against the back of the couch. He propped his feet on the coffee table while Brenna curled one leg beneath her and got comfortable. "Okay, hotshot. Let's go get him."

"First of all, tell me why you accepted the invitation to be on the show. Get beyond the initial flattery to the real reason." She looked at him and waited.

"I decided it would be good publicity for the company," he said promptly.

Brenna's smile would have done Mona Lisa credit. "It's a pleasure to work with you, Matthews," she applauded. "You can't imagine the number of people who don't know why they do these things. And how clearly it shows when they're on the air.

"You want to think of this as a million dollar's worth of free advertising time. Go over your material between now and Friday and decide what main points you want to leave with the listeners. Number them in order of importance."

Kane blinked slowly then stared over her shoulder at the wall. She could practically hear his brain click into gear. In just a few seconds, he was back, waiting for more.

"When Kramer introduces you, he'll tell the audience the name of your company. It's up to you to mention it several more times during the interview."

Kane nodded.

"Never," she emphasized, "repeat a negative comment. Rephrase the question, and rephrase it the way you want to answer it. Try things like, 'If you look at my record, you'll find...' whatever. Or, 'If I understand you correctly, you want to know...' Always answer in the positive."

"Go on," he said quietly.

"This is where those main points come in. Kramer throws you a question and you decide which point most closely answers the question, then you slip it in as smooth as butter."

The corners of Kane's mouth slowly curved up. "I'm beginning to think I might enjoy this after all."

Brenna grinned. "If he starts playing dirty pool, you might be able to throw him off balance. He'll sit back and wait for you to trip over your own tongue. You've seen him do it on some of the tapes. You *have* watched all the tapes, haven't you?" she demanded suspiciously.

Kane's smile grew broader. "Yeah, boss, I have."

"Okay, then you know what I mean. He gets that nauseating smile on his face and pounces. You toss him the shortest answer you can think of and smile right back. Don't say another word, and you'll catch him with his pants down. Then you'll have the fun of watching *him* get rattled and paw through his notes to find his next question."

The thought of turning the tables on Kramer seemed to intrigue Kane, Brenna noted with satisfaction. "Of course, you could take it one more step. It should be a snap for you. If you have something you want to say, take control of the interview while he's fumbling. Be aggressive. Don't wait to be asked. Be controversial. The audience will love you."

"Are you saying that I'm the aggressive type?"

Brenna looked pleadingly at the ceiling, then smiled at Kane's rumble of laughter.

"How bad would it be for Kramer if I did something like that?"

"He'd just have a little egg on his face. Do you really care?"

"No."

"That's what I thought."

Kane looked at his watch and frowned. "Anything else?"

"Yeah. Have you noticed that Kramer often lets a guest expound at length and then, when they're finished, he just lets the answer hang in the air for about ten seconds? Most people assume that they didn't fully answer the question, and they start all over again, fumbling for words and looking foolish. Don't fall for it. Keep your answers punchy, no more than three or five sentences. When you're finished, stop. And smile. Let him worry about the silence. Okay?"

"More than okay," he said quietly.

"I think that's enough for now," Brenna told him. She could tell by his abstracted expression that he was already mentally reorganizing his material.

"I've got to go," he told her, taking another look at his watch.

"Where are you meeting?"

Kane told her the name of a well-known restaurant about ten minutes away. Brenna tucked her arm through his and walked him to the door. "We always tell our clients to be early. If you hurry, you might still get there first."

She stood at the door, waved when he turned back for one last look and watched his car ease away from the curb. It faded from sight and still she leaned against the door-jamb, deep in thought.

Something vital had changed between them during Kane's brief visit, she acknowledged. And if she knew it, she'd bet a data base—whatever *that* was—that Kane did, too. In fact, he had undoubtedly engineered the whole thing.

Of course he had. Did she really believe that he had come over to show her his suit?

Hardly.

Her eyes narrowed in thought. Somehow, sometime during the past few weeks of "open and honest" togeth-erness, he had conditioned her to his touch.

With characteristic honesty, she admitted that he wouldn't have gotten away with it if she had seriously ob-jected. The problem was, she reflected moodily, that she wanted Kane to win. She wanted to find a way to live with him without being swamped by him. She wanted *him*. The only problem she had was that she didn't know how to have him and a life of her own at the same time. And that scared the living daylights out of her.

Even so, she had all but purred and climbed all over him when he's strung kisses down her nape. And Kane was no fool. He undoubtedly knew he'd all but won.

Turning into the house, she thought with a rueful grin that she wasn't ready to surrender, but she was certainly willing to listen!

Early Friday afternoon, Julie swung open the door of Brenna's office and stuck her head in. "I'm off. Anything you need before I go?"

Brenna raised her head and smiled. Julie wore a bold yellow dress and almost vibrated with energy. "It's a good thing you're not working on the computer in that," she said dryly. "You'd probably cause a power surge. By the way, did you remember to shut it off?"

"Yes, it won't growl at you as you walk by." She came in and perched on the corner of Brenna's desk. "I don't know how you can still be so intimidated by that machine. In fact, I still haven't figured out how you got a degree in business without learning about computers."

"It wasn't easy, but I managed."

Grinning, Julie said, "I had high hopes that Kane was going to be a good influence on you."

"On the contrary. He completely demoralized me the other day."

"What on earth did he do?"

"Told me that floppy disks come down with viruses."

Julie shuddered. "Don't even mention the word. I just read about it in a science magazine and—"

"Science fiction?" Brenna asked hopefully. Maybe he *had* been kidding.

"Science, period. They're deadly. From what I understand, they just eat up everything on the disk." Scooting off the desk, she asked idly, "Why was Kane talking about it?"

"I foolishly asked him to tell me what he does at work."

"Oh, well, he had to find out about your fatal flaw sometime, I suppose. What *does* he do?"

"Right now, he's trying to cure the virus."

"The man goes up in my estimation every time you open your mouth. Do you realize what kind of a brain he must have to concentrate on something like that and manage to drive you crazy at the same time? And if he *does* develop something, do you have any idea what that'll mean? He'll be rich."

Brenna thought a moment. "Richer."

"And famous. He'll be a modern day savior," Julie said flatly. "Big business and governments from all over the world will be courting him. Add that to the fact that for sheer sexiness he rates right up there among the tens, and what have you got? One magnificent male. Brenna, are you sure you even know what you want? So what if he comes on a little strong, what's a little control between lovers? Anyway, you've got so much, you could give up a barrelful and never miss it. I know a lot of women who would love to be a doormat for him."

"That's not what he wants!"

"Well, what's the problem, then?"

Brenna's green eyes were shadowed. "Things were different for you. I don't think you could ever completely understand."

"I wonder if *you* really do," Julie countered softly, the concern in her voice was reflected in her eyes.

The two women stared at each other across the width of the desk.

"Julie—"

"Brenna—"

They both broke the heavy silence at the same time, stopped and tried again.

Julie was faster. "I'm sorry, Brenna. Not for interfering, we've both always done that. But for my rotten timing. You don't need any lectures right now. You'll work it out, and whatever you decide, I'll be here to celebrate with you."

They hugged, smiling in relief.

After they broke apart, Julie stopped in the doorway and got in the last word. "Just let me know what we're celebrating—keeping him or letting him go."

Brenna listened to her rapid footsteps until the outer door closed softly. Julie was right. If she were a rational, mature adult, she would accept her childhood experience for what it was and get on with her life. It didn't do a bit of good to agonize over something that had happened so long ago. Anyway, what she had experienced before moving in with Gram was small potatoes compared to what some kids had gone through.

It didn't matter what the rational, mature part of her mind thought. For her, Brenna MacKay, those years had been awful. Watching her mother go from man to man, watching her disappear in the shadow of each man, desperate to please him, had been frightening and had left a legacy of fear that wasn't easy to overcome. In fact, she often wondered if she ever would.

She admitted it was stupid. But she knew that as long as she still reacted like that, she wasn't ready to put herself into someone else's hands. No matter how sexy, smart, or rich they were. Or how much they cared for her.

No, she thought bleakly, it was quite clear that the only one she could trust to keep her life exactly as she wanted it was Brenna MacKay. And if that life was lonely at times, she had plenty of interests, and certainly enough work to keep her busy. In fact, she decided after a quick glance at her watch, if she didn't apply herself to some of that work, she wouldn't be ready when Kane came.

Ten

_____

Are you telling me that he still isn't there?'' Brenna stopped doodling on her notepad and clenched her hand around the telephone receiver in frustrated anger. She took another look at her watch. It was ten after five; Kane's appointment had been for three.

"Yes," an uncertain young voice told her. "I mean, no."

Brenna exhaled sharply and took a deep breath, hoping it would calm her down. It didn't. "Which is it?"

"Yes, I'm telling you, and no, he isn't here." The answer came in a breathy feminine whisper; the speaker clearly wished she had more felicitous news. "He hasn't been in the office for hours."

"Are you Mr. Matthews's secretary?" Brenna asked. The voice didn't sound a bit like the composed contralto that had handled her one previous call to Kane's office.

"No." The single word implied that a fervent "Thank God!" was remaining unspoken. "I was sent over here to take messages for Ms Covington."

The missing Ms Covington was obviously the secretary. If she could be found, she might know the whereabouts of her elusive boss. "Is there any way you can reach Ms Covington?"

"No. I think she's with Mr. Matthews. At least they left together."

Brenna blinked. "Oh."

The image of a statuesque brunette, hair sleeked back in a chignon, walking out the door with Kane, slid into her mind with ridiculous ease. She didn't know what Ms Covington looked like, but the picture suited the absent secretary's husky voice, Brenna decided. The idea depressed her, but in the next moment common sense took over. Kane was busy outwitting a virus, it told her briskly. He didn't have any more time to play games with his secretary then she did to run off to Las Vegas for a week. Whether or not he had the inclination was another matter entirely.

"Do you want to leave a message?"

The thread of impatience weaving through the words drew Brenna away from her gloomy conjecture.

"How much longer are you going to be there?" she asked.

"Everyone leaves here at five-thirty."

"No. No message. Thank you."

Brenna cradled the receiver. What was there to say? He wasn't there; that indicated something about his priorities. A surge of anger, sudden and fierce, encompassing all her doubts and frustration, shook her. Damn it, he could have called. He could have had *that* much consideration. She could have rescheduled some appointments, done the laundry, scrubbed down the kitchen walls, anything! Anything, that is, but what she *had* been doing for the past two hours and fifteen minutes: imagining him in the hospital emergency room for various reasons, up to and including car accidents, heart attacks and injuries inflicted by unknown assailants.

What was even more infuriating was that she had wasted a couple of perfectly good seconds worrying about Kane leaving with a dishy, over developed brunette. "No, not worrying," she told herself crankily, dropping her pencil on the desk and walking over to the door. Thinking, maybe. Considering the possibility. But worrying? Ridiculous! If he wanted to play footsie with an Amazon, fine. It was his choice. He was old enough to know what he was doing. The Amazon was probably even older.

This was the final straw, Brenna decided, refusing even to consider the fact that she might be looking for an easy way out of her relationship with Kane. She wasn't a masochist; she just didn't need this kind of grief. What she was, was mad and she intended to stay that way. Besides, she thought cravenly, it was much easier to argue with Kane when she was mad enough to throttle him. Historically her record of wins with him wasn't very impressive. If they got into another discussion on the subject of control and trust, she'd more than likely wind up agreeing to some preposterous plan again.

She slammed the office door behind her and repeated the satisfying process when she walked into the living room. Damn the man! Two months ago, before she had even heard of Kane Matthews, her future had been predictable, her present peaceful, organized and...

Dull?

The thought was as unexpected and disturbing as Kane's advent into her life had been. Nonsense, she told herself staunchly, walking through to the bedroom and throwing open the closet door. Her business had supplied all the excitement she needed. Before Kane, her life had been serene. Orderly. A calm stream flowing gently over the rocks in her life.

Dull.

She snatched a pair of white jeans and a red V-necked sweater from hangers and tossed them on the bed. Okay, she admitted silently, wiggling out of her skirt and tossing it on the bed beside the jeans, in retrospect—compared to the way things were now—it had been a little dull. But there was nothing wrong with dull. It was a perfectly respectable word. Just a little . . .

Dull.

Brenna tugged on the jeans and slid the silky, loose-knit sweater over her head. A quick shimmy of her hips settled it in place. She slid her feet into sandals, looked around for her purse, checked to make sure her keys were in it and marched to the door. This was it. The Kane Matthews stage of her life was over, finished, kaput.

He had no right to barge in and, and—what? she wondered as she slipped into her car and merged with the traffic heading north toward Del Mar. Bring her a lot of aggravation? Exactly. Kane Matthews had added new dimensions to words like persistence and aggression—not to mention provoke and peeve. She eased her foot up on the gas pedal, remembering the wicked gleam in his eyes when he'd admired her "birthmark."

And Kane took where other men stopped to ask. No other man had made her face up to her own sensuality. No other man had demanded that she take what she wanted from him. No other man had shown her the shattering joy of being a woman.

But damn it, he still had no right—especially since in order to keep what she had found, she had to surrender something almost as dear. It shouldn't have to be that way. A person shouldn't have to give up one part of her life to gain another. Besides, if Kane was the type to take off after an overblown, aging brunette who was probably all wrong for him, she was well rid of him.

Three hours later, after Brenna had repeated and exhausted every argument she could dredge up for ending an affair that was more properly called a relationship, Kane finally drove into his street. From her car, parked two doors away, she watched his garage door open, hesitate and swing down. Moments later, lights in the windows pinpointed Kane's progress through the lower floor of the house.

Brenna took a deep breath, stepped from her car and walked up to Kane's door. Resolutely she pressed her finger to the bell then stepped back to wait.

When Kane opened the door, she noticed he hadn't had a chance to do much more than drop his briefcase and remove his jacket and tie. The first two buttons of his shirt were open and his sleeves were rolled up to his forearms. He looked down at her without a trace of expression.

His distant look fanned the flames of Brenna's anger. There wasn't even a glimmer of recognition on his face. Fine, she decided, moving from mad to furious in the blink of an eyelash, she didn't need a truck to fall on her. If he was ready to move on to someone else, if he preferred the brunette, fine. He could have her—heavy haunches and all. She drew in a quick breath and began her enraged little speech.

"The first time I tried to do this," she said stiffly, "I le you a note. It would have been better for you'd—no, I'm not going to get into that, forget it. Since then, I've learned my lesson. No more notes. So here it is in plain English. I won't—''

Kane blinked slowly—twice—and Brenna had the strangest feeling that she was watching him return from some distant place.

''—be seeing you anymore,'' she continued, eyeing him warily. ''It just isn't working.''

He blinked again and she found herself staring into eyes that had lost their abstraction and were focusing intently on her frosty expression. Kane wasn't a man who gave much away, but for once Brenna knew exactly what he was thinking. She saw the jolt of recognition in his eyes when he actually *saw* her, and knew exactly when he remembered their appointment. Fine lines at the corners of his eyes contracted in a wince of remorse, followed by a flare of anxiety and concern.

''Oh, hell,'' he said disgustedly. He swore briefly with a virtuosity that stirred a distant chord of admiration in Brenna.

She listened politely until he was through. ''I couldn't agree more,'' she agreed coldly and turned on her heel to leave. Kane wrapped his hand around her upper arm and stopped her before she had taken two steps.

''I forgot,'' he said simply.

''I noticed.''

Wincing again, he said, ''Yeah, I suppose you did.''

''Let me go, Kane.''

''Not until we talk.''

''—?'' she said furiously, prying at her fingers. ''—, brunettes? Get your hands off me. I don't —n't want to listen. I want to get in my car — want you to call me, and if you do, I —'' Her enraged spatter of words ended in a small shriek as Kane wrapped a long arm around her waist and hoisted her over the doorstep.

"Calm down, you little hellcat." He grunted, taking an elbow in his ribs.

"Let . . . me . . . go!"

Kane kicked the heavy door shut and set her on her feet in the entryway.

Brenna didn't stop to consider the odds of winning a fight with a man twice her size, she just drew back her arm and swung.

Kane didn't stop to reason with her. He ducked and moved in closer. When he stood up, Brenna was draped over his shoulder, her fists pounding harmlessly on his back. He tightened his grip on the backs of her thighs and headed for the stairs.

"Damn you," she panted, grabbing his belt and hanging on. "I'll get you for this if it's the last thing I ever do."

Kane took the steps two at a time and didn't let her down until he was in the living room. He set her on her feet and stepped back out of range. She just stood there, shaking with fury, her eyes shooting emerald slivers of ice at him. He wanted to smooth back her tumbled hair but decided that he just might lose a hand if he tried.

Instead he dragged one through his own hair. "Lady, if this is the way you get when I'm late, what would you do if I didn't show up at all?"

Brenna took a deep, ragged breath. "For your information," she said icily, "missing an appointment by five and a half hours isn't late, it *is* not showing up."

"Five hours?" he said incredulously. He looked down at his watch in disbelief.

"Oh, come on. Give me a break." Brenna drenched the words with skepticism and stalked around him and over to the window overlooking the deck. She jammed her hands into the back pockets of her jeans and forced her gaze downward to the water below, hoping that the peaceful scene would slow down the adrenaline coursing through her body. She concentrated on taking another deep breath, trying to ignore the blood that was still pounding, pressing against skin that was tight and prickly.

"It's almost eight-thirty," Kane said.

She made a frustrated sound at his stunned tone and whirled around. "Tell me something I don't know," she suggested.

He looked at the wall clock for confirmation then back at his watch. "It can't be," he stated flatly.

"Didn't the setting sun glaring in your eyes on the way home give you a small clue?" she asked.

After a short silence, Kane said, "I didn't notice it."

"Didn't—?" Brenna stopped, speechless for a moment. "Kane, you drove right into it. It had to be blinding."

"I was . . . thinking."

"*Thinking?* I'd say you were in a coma."

"Yeah." He ran his hand through his hair again. "That happens sometimes when I get involved in things," he said vaguely.

She moved a couple of steps closer. "Let me get this straight. Are you telling me that you were concentrating on something and lost track of time?"

He shrugged, a sheepish grin kicking up one corner of his mouth. "Yeah, I guess that's what I'm saying."

Brenna narrowed her eyes. "Nobody," she said belligerently, "gets that involved in anything."

He raised his brows and looked at her, wondering if she was going to come any closer. "I lost a whole day once."

She made an exasperated sound deep in her throat and briefly looked up at the ceiling. "I'm still furious," she said, pacing over to the coffee table.

"I don't blame you," he said promptly. "You have every right to be. Being five hours—"

"Five and a half."

"—five and a half hours late is inexcusable. If you had a lick of sense, you'd—"

"Oh, shut . . . up."

Brenna scowled at him ferociously. He was doing it again, she reflected in alarm. With just a few words he had defused the anger pumping through her. Any minute now, he'd be coaxing a smile out of her. Why? she wondered yet again. Why this man? There must be hundreds, thousands of men whom she would find compatible and not nearly so unsettling. Why did she have to want the one man who could drive her into an appalling rage one minute and have her fighting a smile the next? And on a scale of one to ten, why did he have to be a twelve in bed? Life just wasn't fair.

Kane moved around the table until he was standing next to her. "I'm sorry, honey. I know it's a rotten excuse, but I forgot."

"You're right, it's rotten. And it doesn't make me feel any better," she said coolly, staring down at the fireplace. "And don't call me honey."

There was a heavy silence while they both examined the marble hearth. Finally Kane said bluntly, "Brenna, I've lived alone for a lot of years. I'm not used to calling home and telling someone I'll be late."

Brenna stared at him, almost dizzy with anger, hardly believing what she had heard. "Let's get one thing straight," she snapped. "I wasn't sitting at anyone's home waiting for you. I'm neither your wife nor your live-in lover. I was in my office and you had an appointment with me. Do you treat all your business associates like that, or am I singled out for the dubious honor?"

"Damn it, Brenna!" Kane scowled down at her in frustration. What he had done was stupid and unforgivable, he reminded himself, so he'd better cool down and give her the time she needed. Especially if he was going to put a size eleven foot in his mouth every time he opened it. He watched her moodily, surprised by the strength of his desire—no, his need—for her understanding and forgiveness. And he would get it when he had a chance to explain. But first she deserved the opportunity to throw a few punches—verbal, not the kind she had attempted downstairs, he amended wryly.

Someday, when she wasn't in the mood to slug him, he'd tell her how beautiful she had been at that moment. When her anger had sizzled through the room, something basic and elemental in him had responded. He had staked his claim on her for the final time. If he hadn't been busy ducking, he reflected as a tinge of male possessiveness merged with anticipation, he would have dragged her down on the floor and helped her rechannel that energy in a more basic way.

"And while we're on the subject," Brenna fumed, "in case you don't remember, I live alone, too. Life is much simplier that way. Don't you agree?"

Kane looked at her suspiciously, all indulgence gone. "Now, wait a minute."

"There's only one person to cook for, one person to plan for, one person to... worry about." Brenna sniffed and came to an abrupt stop, damning the emotion that made her voice wobble.

Kane hadn't appeared to move, but suddenly his arm was brushing against hers and she felt his heat all the way down her body.

"Worry?" His voice was gentle.

She shrugged awkwardly and tried to turn away from his searching gaze, but his arm around her shoulder kept her facing him. "Forget it," she muttered, staring straight at the dark chest hair exposed by the open neck of his shirt.

"Worried, Brenna? About me?" There was a surprising vulnerability in his voice that made her look up.

When her eyes reluctantly met his, she nodded. Blinking too-bright eyes, she returned her gaze to the springy patch of hair. "All right," she admitted aggressively, "so I was worried."

"Why?" He tugged her closer and the word rumbled in his chest beneath her cheek.

She sniffed. "I thought you were dead."

"Dead?"

She nodded again, burrowing her nose against his throat.

"Dead?" he repeated blankly, looking down and running a gentle finger along a strand of pale hair that splashed across his shirt.

"I thought you had been in an accident," she explained in a watery mumble. "Or had a heart attack."

"Why?" he asked gently, smoothing the strand of hair into a silky ribbon across his heart. "Wouldn't it have been just as easy to imagine me working?"

Brenna shook her head and pressed her face into his chest.

"Why not, sweetheart?"

"Because," she wept, her voice rising to a soft wail, "I knew that if you were just working, you would have *called* me."

Instinctively Kane tightened his arms, holding Brenna closer, running a soothing hand down her quivering back. Beyond that, his muscles didn't seem to work. Guilt clenched his insides together until he felt as though he had just been kicked in the stomach. During the past few minutes, Brenna had taken him for a ride on an emotional roller coaster that had literally left him breathless. One minute she was as dangerous as a she-bear, the next as vulnerable as a fawn.

Exhaling sharply, Kane shook his head like a punch drunk fighter. He knew how to build a business, he reflected wryly, cupping the back of Brenna's head with his hand and drawing her closer until her nose touched his throat. He could cope with the competition in the cutthroat software world. He could hold his own in a fight. But he was only a man. He had no idea what to do with a crying woman. He could handle her anger; hell, he could glory in it, be aroused by it, but her tears defeated him.

Then, like a spray of fireworks exploding against a canopy of black sky, the realization hit him. The first time he had seen her, he'd known she was going to be his. Everything he had done—forcing himself to be the man she thought she wanted, taking her to bed, keeping two jumps ahead of her crazy plans and implementing a few of his own—had been with one purpose in mind: to have Brenna become a part of his life. But *this*, holding her in his arms while she wept hot tears into his shirt, was the stuff commitments were made of. Holding her naked body against his, making love until they were exhausted, though vital, was only the beginning.

It was the minor, everyday happenings—arguing and making up, worrying about each other's well-being, holding on tight while tears trickled in silvery paths—that forged the bonds of a relationship. Those things fash-

ioned the indestructible links on the chain with which he
wanted to bind the two of them together.

Wondering how he was going to share his insight with
Brenna, Kane shifted his weight. She snuggled closer, distracting him when her breasts pressed warmly and sweetly
into his chest. How could he tell her that he wanted the
entire range of her feminine artillery aimed at him? That
he didn't want her tears dripping down the neck of any
other man's shirt? That if ambulance sirens were going to
conjure up pictures of loved ones dying, he wanted her
worrying about *him*?

Kane sighed. He didn't know. But he would, soon.

He nuzzled her cheek and trailed his lips down the soft
line of her jaw.

Brenna stirred. "Don't do that," she ordered in a soggy
voice. "I'm still mad."

"I don't blame you," he murmured, dropping a small
kiss on the exact center of her chin.

She turned her face and grumbled softly, "I don't like
you very much right now."

"But you love this." His teeth closed gently over her
velvety earlobe, his breath warm on her temple.

Brenna's eyes snapped open. "Damn it, Kane!"

"And this." His mouth touched the agitated pulse in the
hollow of her throat.

"Kane." It was a weak warning.

"And this." His lips settled in the sweet juncture of her
neck and shoulder.

"Uh..."

"And this." He picked her up and took the few steps to
the couch. Dropping down, he settled her in his lap and
touched his lips to the point on her shoulder where the
neck of her sweater began its downward plunge.

"Ummmm."

"And this."

"Oh!"

"And this."

"Yes, damn it."

"Good."

She looked up at him. "Don't look so satisfied with yourself. You still make me furious."

"That's all part of it, babe." He set her on the cushion beside him. A few seconds later he was stretched out next to Brenna, her head resting on his shoulder.

"I was working," he said abruptly. "It's not much of an excuse, but it's the truth. One of the men called from the lab. They had hit a snag and I went down to see what I could do. I took Laura—"

Brenna arched her brows. "Laura?"

"—my secretary, with me so she could take notes. I didn't think I'd be down there long, but things got...involved and I lost track of the time. I also forgot to have anyone call you."

With an overly casual yawn, Brenna asked, "Did you all stay so late?"

"Most of us. Laura left early because she had to collect her grandson from preschool."

"Oh."

"Why? Afraid I'm going to be charged with using slave labor?"

Brenna's smile almost blinded him. "No." She didn't elaborate. "What was the problem in the lab?"

"The virus," he said, examining the smile cautiously.

"Did you solve it?"

"No. Logically, it should..." He broke off, frowning at the wall. "We worked until we started making stupid mistakes, then we called it quits. We're that close," he raised his hand, finger and thumb almost touching, "to a break-through."

"You'll do it," she said comfortably, smiling when he resumed frowning at the wall. So there was no brunette secretary. And he was neither dead nor dying. He had been *thinking*, for God's sake. Brenna blinked, unable even to imagine such powers of concentration. He didn't remember driving home and he'd been in another world when he'd opened the door. He hadn't even recognized her.

"What brunette?" Kane asked suddenly.

One quick, silent groan was all Brenna allowed herself. Then she rounded her eyes innocently and said, "Hmm?"

"After I opened the door and you gave your touching farewell speech, you asked if I wanted to talk about brunettes." He never took his eyes off her.

"Are you sure?" she said doubtfully, disciplining her expression.

"Yeah, I'm sure."

"Oh. Why on earth would I say a thing like that?"

Kane raised himself up on his elbow and looked down at her, taking in the slight pink flush on her face and the green eyes that stubbornly refused to meet his. He dropped back down and said blandly, "I can't imagine."

Brenna relaxed her tense muscles and smiled.

"Unless you were jealous."

"What?" She jerked, attempting to sit up, but his hand on her shoulder kept her right where she was—right where he could watch every flicker of expression that crossed her face.

He smiled complacently. "Jealous."

"Ridiculous!" She packed as much scorn as she could into the one word.

"Is it?"

He looked like a cat that had just licked cream off its whiskers, Brenna thought in disgust. "Yes, it is. I don't even know a brunette who knows you."

"Maybe not. But we both know what an imagination you have, don't we? You had me dead and buried this afternoon, why not add taking off with a gorgeous brunette to the agenda?" He took another look at her face and chuckled.

"You sound very pleased with yourself," she said crossly, looking up into caressing gray eyes.

He leaned down and kissed the tip of her nose. "I am. It makes me feel like a, a . . ."

"Superstud?" she asked nastily.

He grinned. "Yeah, exactly."

Brenna groaned.

After a moment, Kane lost his smile and said grimly, "If the situation had been reversed this afternoon and my thoughts had turned in that direction, I'd have been as jealous as hell."

Her eyes widening, Brenna said, "You would?"

"Yes, and I would have done the same thing you did. I would have hunted you down."

Brenna moistened her dry lips with the tip of her tongue. "And then what?"

"I would have brought you back where you belong. Right here."

"I don't live here," she pointed out breathlessly.

He just looked at her. "I didn't say where you live, I said where you belong."

Stirring restlessly, Brenna said, "I think that's something we need to talk about."

Kane sat up, bringing Brenna along with him. Hell, he thought gloomily. After the day he'd had, he wasn't sure he was up to keeping a couple of steps ahead of Brenna in a serious discussion. Besides, he wasn't ready to let her go. But he did it anyway, before he said, "I know you like your place, but this house is bigger than yours."

Brenna turned to face him, resting her arm along the back of the couch. "But it's not my house."

"I'm offering to make it ours," he said gently.

"Oh, Kane." She sighed. "Don't you understand? It's more than which roof we're under. It's the kind of people we are. I'm afraid—"

"Of *me*?" he interrupted in disbelief.

Eleven

He was hurt. In that split second before he turned his face away and left her gazing at his set profile, Brenna saw the shock in his eyes.

"How could you think I'd ever—"

She rushed to stop him, to comfort, to heal. Touching his cheek with gentle fingers, she said in a soft voice, "Kane, I didn't mean it that way. Oh, darling, I know you'd never hurt me." Not deliberately.

Oh, damn! She frowned, furious with herself for putting that stony, *wounded* look on his face. Where was his blasted macho image when she needed it? She could batter away at him when he was doing his Atilla the Hun routine, but how could she fight a man who was so openly vulnerable? Especially when she was probably one of the few people in the world who saw him that way?

Then, in one of those maddening, rapid-fire changes he excelled at, he turned back to her and raised an interested eyebrow. "Darling?" he asked.

Brenna scowled. "You recover fast," she said dryly.

He reached out for her hand, raised it slowly to his mouth and dropped a kiss in her palm. Closing her fingers over it, he said complacently, "You convinced me." He reached out, collected her and drew her up against him, then looked down at her with pleased speculation. "Darling?" he said again.

"You were testing me," Brenna accused, narrowing her eyes.

Kane shook his head, the teasing gleam disappearing from his eyes. "No, that's one thing I couldn't joke about." He exhaled sharply. "If you didn't mean—"

She touched his hand lightly, tracing his knuckles with her thumb. "Kane," she began slowly, searching for the right words, "It's not just you. It's me. I'm not much of a risk taker."

He stiffened. "Would loving me be such a risk?"

She saw it again, that flash of pain. "It could be," she said starkly.

"Why?" He laced his fingers through hers, holding her when she tried to draw back.

Brenna looked down. Somehow their linked hands seemed symbolic. His large one was harder, tougher, stronger. Dominant. Then she blinked thoughtfully, remembering how he had cared for her when she was sick, how his hands had gentled her, tenderly soothed her aching body. And how, in this very room, those same hands had created and appeased an entirely different sort of ache.

"I don't know if I can make you understand," she said reluctantly. "It sounds so...petty when I put it into words."

He nudged her companionably with his shoulder. "I'm listening."

Brenna burrowed the back of her head into his chest and sighed. Would she ever understand him, she wondered. In the blink of an eye he could turn an ordinary conversation into seduction, and now, when she expected anger, he offered encouragement.

"I need to know that I'm in charge of my own life. I've worked for years to build what I have," she finally told him. "To be independent, to make my own decisions. No one told me to settle in this area, and no one will tell me when to move. I still have the same friends I made when I came to this part of the state, and I plan to keep them for a long, long time. Julie and I created A Touch of Class the same way—our own way. When we made mistakes, they were *our* mistakes, no one else's. And now we're settled, established, permanent. We're a part of the community."

She glanced sideways at him. "Do you understand what I'm saying?" she asked anxiously.

He nodded, wondering if she thought he planned to stuff her in a motor home and keep her on the run for the next five years. "So far," he said. "Where does this leave the man in your life?"

"Giving me a lot of space and assuming that I'm capable of making my own decisions."

Kane slanted a wary glance down at the top of Brenna's head. She was doing a lot of fancy footwork around the subject, he thought in relief. Outside of the furious words she'd thrown at him when he opened the door, she hadn't actually told him to get out of her life. That was the good news. The bad was that he'd obviously miscalculated the depth of her resistance.

Did she honestly think that he had the time to sit around and take over the running of her life? he wondered. Or that he wanted to? He had all he could do to keep up with his own business, for God's sake. Besides, he had never been attracted to passive women who coiled around men like parasites, waiting for them to assume the role of dominant male. Although she didn't believe it, Brenna's spirited attack on life was one of the things he liked most about her. And he wouldn't do a thing to curb it.

He shifted, automatically tightening his arm around her, and thought about her house. The way she talked, you'd think he was planning to sell it out from under her. He didn't give a damn where she lived—as long as it was with him.

No, he reflected, the problem went beyond houses and jobs. It had to do with the way Brenna had overreacted the morning after they'd made love. Narrowing his eyes in thought, he compared that to the memory of the two of them in front of the fireplace that night—the exultant look on her face when she'd tossed her inhibitions out the window. She had teased him with hot kisses, tormented him with a body that would inflame a plaster saint. And then the following night she had the gall to tell him that she wasn't a sensual woman.

Kane winced. The trouble with applying logic to an emotional problem was that the answer was often inevitable—and unwelcome. In this case, it was pretty obvious that it wasn't him that Brenna didn't trust—it was herself. And if he was right, there wasn't a damn thing that he could do about it. He could talk until he lost his voice and it wouldn't do a bit of good. Brenna had to deal with this herself.

But he could help—that is, he could if she would just answer some direct questions with even more direct answers. He frowned, staring at the marble hearth.

Before Brenna had time to brood over the various reasons that could be keeping Kane quiet, he surged to his feet, taking her along with him. One of his hands settled on her shoulder, the other clamped gently over her mouth. Her breath was a warm puff against his palm when she looked up, trying to read the expression in his shuttered gray eyes. His grasp was loose and she knew she could have pulled away, but curiosity kept her still. And one other thing; she had never seen Kane rattled or nervous. Right now, he was both.

"Look," Kane said, "We've done a lot of talking in the past few weeks, but in my opinion, we've never even gotten near our real problem. We can cut through a lot of the underbrush if you'll just nod yes or no to a few questions. Will you do it? No other talking, just yes or no?"

Brenna nodded. She hadn't consciously made the decision, the answer was simply there.

At her agreement, he added, "Will you just trust me for a while?"

Brenna nodded again, barely tilting her head.

He cleared his throat. "First of all, I've done my share of talking lately, but I've managed to leave out the most important words of all. I want you, Brenna. But more than that, I *need* you."

Brenna hardly breathed, stunned by the stark yearning in his silvery eyes. Want? Need? she wondered blankly. What about love?

"I have my work," he persevered, touching her silky hair with his fingertips, "but it's not enough. I have a house, but without you it's just four walls and a roof. It's never going to be a home unless you live in it, too. This isn't as selfish as it sounds," he assured her quickly. "I want to make a home for *you*, too. It doesn't have to be this place, if you don't like it. I want to give you everything that I'm looking for myself."

Kane took a deep breath and exhaled sharply. Shaking his head, he muttered disgustedly, "Not the most graceful of declarations, is it? Believe it or not, I've never done this before, and it isn't as easy as it looks."

Brenna's lips curved in a smile against his palm. Her heart swelled as she made note of another first. Kane was awkward and ill at ease. He was also walking a country mile around the word *love*. But then, she admitted, so was she. Before she could pursue that interesting line of thought, Kane took her by surprise again.

He bent his head and deposited a kiss on the tip of her nose. Then he straightened with a lazy grin. Brenna stiffened her spine, ready for almost anything. She didn't trust that look on his face at *all*. He was probably going to push her to the limit, but in the past few weeks she had done crazier things than this and survived. And it just might offer a way out of the hole they'd dug for themselves.

"Now, it's your turn," he told her. "Do you want to settle this as much as I do? Yes or no."

Brenna nodded. Yes.

"You'll answer my questions?"

Brenna sighed and nodded again. Yes.

"At night, when you go to bed would you like me there next to you?"

She stiffened, caught by surprise. She hadn't been prepared for *that*. When she hesitated, his hand tightened on her shoulder. She nodded slowly, grudgingly. Yes.

"Do you ache for me the way I ache for you?"

Narrowing her eyes in warning, her nod was another reluctant yes.

"Do you ever think about forgetting all your problems and just being in my arms, making love?"

Brenna took a deep breath, glaring at him. He really did play dirty. He didn't know the meaning of the word scruple. He was definitely taking advantage of—

Kane's fingers flexed on her shoulder. "Well?"

Her eyes told him what she thought of his tactics, but she nodded. Yes.

"Do you want me, Brenna?" His smile slipped a little as he waited.

Her lashes lowered in exasperation, then lifted. Yes.

"Do you need me in your life as much as I need you in mine?"

She made a sound against his palm, but the stark anxiety in his eyes made her nod. Yes.

Kane closed his eyes and let his breath out in a rush. When he opened them, his gray gaze locked with hers. "Do you trust me, Brenna, in every way that's important?"

Without having to think, she replied in a muffled voice, "Yes."

Still holding her captive, he said gently, "When it comes to loving me, do you trust yourself?"

Stunned, she stared up at him. She couldn't move in the charged silence that followed. Kane's face was taut and grim with strain by the time she hesitantly shook her head back and forth.

Instantly his face relaxed. With a half-grin he said solemnly, "I've got a plan that'll fix that."

Brenna groaned, but she couldn't resist the gathering anticipation in his eyes, the gleam of amusement. Teasingly she touched the tip of her tongue to his palm and smiled with her eyes when he jumped.

His grin grew wider. "I suggest that we settle this once and for all."

Tilting her head, Brenna watched him questioningly.

"By making love."

Brenna closed her eyes and exhaled into his palm. Men! Was this their solution for everything?

Kane laughed. "Wait a minute, give me a chance to finish. This time, *you're* going to be in charge."

Opening one eye, Brenna considered him thoughtfully.

"You'll have control from start to finish. You take it as far as you want, stop when you want. Of course," he explained generously, "if you want to hand over your, ah, authority at any time, I'll be happy to take over for a while. You get the reins back as soon as you want them," he assured her.

Her body let her know which way *it* voted. Waves of need washed over her. Trying to ignore the ache, Brenna eyed him uncertainly, hazily wondering about loopholes and fine print.

She was intrigued. Admit it, she lectured herself, she was hungry for him. As starved as he was. It was also a chance to see whether they could have the love they both wanted without releasing the storm of passion that had so totally overwhelmed her the last time—the one that had scared the daylights out of her. She wasn't asking for much, she reflected wryly. All she wanted was love that was controllable, that wouldn't turn her into a spineless, dependent wilted lily.

"And after we've given it our best shot," Kane finished determinedly, "if you still think it won't work for us, you can walk away and I won't bother you anymore. I promise. The decision will be yours." He moved his hand away from her mouth, touching her lower lip with a gentle thumb. "What do you say, Brenna, yes or no?"

He stood close enough to touch her, but he didn't. He could have pulled her into his arms, but he didn't. Invitation gleamed in his smoky eyes, blatant and enticing, but he didn't say a word while he waited.

Brenna never took her eyes from his while she absorbed what he'd said. Her body clamored for an affirmative reply, clouding her ability to think. By taking away his hand, Kane had removed her option of simply nodding her head. He wanted her answer to stand loud and clear between them. If she said yes, there was hope. And if she said no, she would be walking out the door to emptiness.

Kane finally cleared his throat. "Well?"

"Yes."

"Yes?"

"Yes!"

"Dear God," he breathed, delight warming his eyes, "I've died and gone to heaven. Do you know," he teased, "that ever since I was a kid I've fantasized about being seduced by a leggy blonde?"

"I vaguely remember you mentioning something about that. Too bad we don't have a seedy motel available," she sympathized nervously, wondering just when this latest plan was going into effect. "And that your fantasy blonde is such a...novice." Her eyes were on him in mute appeal.

His wicked smile was anything but reassuring. "Great things are often achieved when begun simply with enthusiasm."

"Who said that?"

"I did."

Brenna shifted restlessly, ridiculously embarrassed. Turning her profile to him, she said, "When do you think we should, ah..."

"Well, you're the lady in charge, but I'd suggest right now." He drew the silence out for a long time, then added, "Before you decide to bolt out the door."

Glaring at him over her shoulder, she said, "I'm not planning to run. I just wondered—"

"Good." He all but rubbed his hands together. "Then I'm going down to take a shower. Want to come?"

"Uh, I'll be along in a minute," she said vaguely.

Whistling softly, Kane turned away. The tuneless little sound drifted up to her as he descended the stairs and went into his bedroom. It continued as two shoes hit the floor with small thumps and finally disappeared when the bathroom door was closed softly.

A couple of things galvanized Brenna into action. First of all, she wasn't ready to peel off her clothes in front of Kane while he stood around naked and damp and watched with a great deal of interest—and that's exactly what she'd be doing if she stalled much longer. In addition to that—regardless of the outcome of this crazy scheme—she couldn't wait to get her hands on him! She pulled her sweater over her head and was unhooking her bra as she ran down the stairs.

Less than a minute later, she opened the shower door and stepped in. Kane was standing under a pulsating stream of water, not moving a muscle. One more step brought her beside him and she nudged him over with her hip.

"*Aaahhh!* The water's cold," she yelped, all thoughts of seduction momentarily abandoned.

"If I'm going to make it as far as the bedroom, I need all the help I can get," he said simply.

As she edged out of the cold stream, her gaze worked its way down his body, following the dark trail of hair that narrowed at his flat stomach, then abruptly widened. She put out her hand and slowly traced the hairline back up to his chest, then rested her hands on his shoulders. Taking a second downward glance and primming her mouth, she agreed, "Ah, yes. You do seem to have a problem. A big one."

A chuckle shook his frame and he wrapped his arms around her waist, tugging her against him. Brenna reached out and fiddled with the faucet until the water was warm.

"That's not going to help," he warned.

"I'm new at this," she reminded him. "Besides, I told you, I learn from my mistakes."

"Oh. Well, in that case..." He bent down, teasing her lips with his own, sliding his hand down to her hips and over the enticing fullness of her bottom.

"Enthusiasm," she confided between kisses, "is a wonderful thing." She stood on tiptoe, her arms circling his neck. The rigid evidence of his arousal rested against her stomach. "There are quite a few things...I've never done with a...man before," she told him, touching her lips to the deep crease in his cheek.

"Umm."

"For starters, I've never...made love in a shower... before."

Kane lifted his head, breathing fast, a complicated gleam of heat and amusement in his eyes. He lifted his hand and with his thumb gently stroked the hard bead of her nipple. "Is that right?"

Brenna sucked in her breath and shook her head. "Never."

One large hand settled on the smooth curve of her stomach and his lips touched hers again in light, nipping kisses. "At least...once in your life...you should—"

"That's what I thought," she gasped, burying her face against his shoulder. "Uh, if I were to turn things over to you for a while, I suppose you'd—"

"Know what to do," he assured her between clenched teeth.

"Good."

Brenna sagged against him, brushing a string of kisses across his chest while he gently nudged her thighs apart and touched her.

"My God, honey, you're a living invitation."

"Enthusiasm," she murmured faintly.

"Enthusiasm, hell," Kane muttered. "You're hot. And wet. And waiting. For me." He lifted her up against the water-warmed tiles, brushing his mouth across her breast, his tongue curling around the pebble-hard nipple. When Brenna gasped, he lowered her, sliding into the tight, silky sheath of her body.

"Oh, babe," he murmured thickly, "I wanted to wait, but I don't think I can. Wrap your legs around me."

Brenna obeyed with a small moan, encircling his neck with her arms, her instinctive movement bringing him closer, deeper.

"Oh!" It was a ragged moan. "I didn't know—"

He stood braced and rigid, waiting for her body to adjust to his, exulting in her disjointed words and breathless cries.

"Kane!"

"Umm?"

"Ahh."

"Yeah."

"It's so—"

"I know."

Brenna's fingers worked restlessly through his thick hair, shaping, clinging, touching, stroking. The movement tightened her body and Kane felt the first, featherlight tremor ripple through her.

With each passing moment, the tiny convulsive shimmer became stronger, more insistent, matching their spasmodic gasps for air. Drowning in waves of pleasure,

Brenna clung to Kane, matching his thrusting movements with demands of her own, again and again until she shuddered in release, drawing the warmth of his love deep within her. His arms chained her to him and she heard him repeat her name over and over. Claiming. Possessing.

Brenna slumped against him, her pounding heart slowly returning to normal. Kane's breathing was deep and ragged, his arms still holding her tight against him. Then he slowly lifted her and carefully set her on her feet. Brenna blinked up at him, instinctively reaching out, wrapping her arms around his waist and fitting herself against his body. He turned his back to the pounding water, protecting her from its force, tightening his arm around her waist when she sighed and tucked her head beneath his chin.

Kane let out a deep breath, his hand shaping itself for a luxuriant moment to the flare of her hip. He looked down at the water-slick bundle of femininity he held and understood for the first time why men were possessive and territorial, why challenges were issued and accepted, why men fought savagely for the right to claim a particular woman. His lips curving in a small, very masculine smile, he reached for the soap.

When he began working the lather down her back and over the rounded curve of her bottom, Brenna looked up.

"Wow." Her eyes were round and stunned.

Kane grinned lazily. "Yeah."

She stepped back, giving him access to the rest of her body, purring as he massaged and stroked every inch of it. When he was finished, she stepped beneath the spray, lifted her arms and let the silvery stream wash away the creamy foam. Then she turned, the corners of her mouth lifting in a tormenting little smile and reached for the bar of soap.

"My turn."

The two small words were enough. Kane understood that by uttering them, Brenna was reestablishing control. And if the expression in her eyes was any indication, she was going to do her best to drive him crazy. His smile grew broader. God only knew he was willing to take whatever she dished out—if he could stand it.

Even as he looked down at her, watching as she replaced the soap and meticulously spread a mound of lather over his chest, he felt his body tighten. Sensual need swept through him like rolling clouds gathering for a storm, funnelling the small electric darts of anticipation straight to his groin.

With the air of an artist creating a masterpiece, Brenna sculptured the frothy soap over slabs of muscle, smoothing it on his stomach as she followed the narrowing line of dark, springy hair. Her hand slowed, then came to a complete stop as her fingers gently explored the soft flesh low on his stomach. Kane's groan was as involuntary as the convulsive movement of his body.

Brenna's gaze dropped, then slowly moved up to meet the wry expression in his smoky eyes. "I thought we took care of that," she said in mock surprise.

Kane chuckled, the sound reverberating through the small enclosure. "How long are you going to keep this torture up?" He spoke to the top of her head since she was now on her knees before him, intently applying lather to the inside of his thigh.

"I've never done this before, either," she said reasonably, as if that explained everything.

Sucking air in between his teeth, he waited for her small hand to slide a notch higher. When it move contrarily down toward his knee, he exhaled slowly—also between his teeth. "I hate to spoil your fun," he said grittily as her hand slid up his other thigh, "but I'm warning you that I don't always have complete control over these things."

"Are you begging for mercy?" she asked, her eyes bright with interest.

His hands dropped heavily on her shoulders. "Let's just say that you'd be wise to take my warning at face value."

"Okay, okay," she mumbled, getting to her feet. She stood in front of him, rinsing the lacy soap bubbles off her arms and hands. When she was satisfied with the results, she turned the hot water tap down and stepped close to the shower head, letting the water dart past her onto Kane's chest.

"Damn it!" he roared, "it's freezing!"

She looked at him with wide, innocent eyes. "Sorry. I thought that would help." Before she had finished, he was gone.

Smiling, she turned the hot water back on, closed her eyes and allowed herself one last moment of undisturbed luxury. Finally, humming contentedly, she reached for the tap—and found her hand resting on Kane's. She opened her eyes and saw him leaning against the glass doorway, a towel knotted casually at his hips.

"I thought you might need some help," he said blandly, tugging her gently out of the shower and draping a towel around her shoulders.

The next few minutes were a revelation to Brenna. She had never realized exactly how seductive a towel could be in the hands of an inventive man. Eyelashes lowered, she abandoned herself to the pleasurable sensation of the softly abrasive fabric brushing her nipples, stroking her from head to toe. Shock waves of need were washing over her by the time Kane was satisfied.

He got to his feet, skimming the towel from her ankle to her nape, then dropping a swift kiss on her parted lips. He patted her bottom proprietarily and draped the towel around her like a sarong, tucking the corner down the shadowy V between her breasts. Threading his fingers through hers, he led her through the bedroom to an upholstered, double-size lounge chair in the corner of the room. He stopped only once, near the door, to turn on a small lamp sitting on the dresser.

He nudged her down on the cushion then sprawled beside her, turning her to face him.

"Nice," she murmured, rubbing her head against his shoulder until it felt just right. "What are we doing here?"

"Resting," he said succinctly, "until you decide what else you have up your sleeve. Remember, you're the lady in charge."

They lay in comfortable silence, content for the moment to simply be near, to hold each other, to touch. And doze.

Later Kane opened his eyes, fully aware that his body was reacting to Brenna's nearness. It wasn't surprising, he reflected a moment later. She was even closer than he'd realized. Her slim fingers were weaving a pattern through the mat of hair on his chest, stopping every now and then to test the hardness of his flat nipple.

"You awake?" she whispered.

"Umm."

She shifted a bit closer. "I just thought of something."

"Let me guess." She could hear the smile in his voice. "You've never made love in a lounge chair."

Twelve

————

Brenna chuckled drowsily. "How'd you guess?"

"I'm beginning to understand how your mind works." His voice was a contented rumble.

"Do you think I'm going to become addicted to this?" she wondered aloud, her voice a soft purr.

"God, I hope so!" He propped himself up on one elbow and encouraged her with fleeting touches of his lips, starting at her earlobe, then grazing the delicate ridge of her collarbone and finally settling on the high, firm swell of her breast. He reached out and painstakingly withdrew the corner of the towel from between her breasts. With his fingertips, he gently nudged the fabric aside.

"Did I ever tell you how much I enjoy unwrapping packages?" The dark pleasure in his eyes took Brenna's breath away.

Instead of answering, she trailed her fingers down the center of his chest until she reached the towel that was covering him. Detouring to the right, she soon found the knot at his hips and made short work of it.

"Lift up for a second, love," Kane directed, impatient with the sheet of fabric separating them. When she did, he pulled it out from beneath her and dropped it on the floor. A second later, he did the same to his.

His arms wrapped around her, pulling her against him until the length of her body knew the imprint of every inch of his. The prickly hair on his thighs gently rasped her legs as he raised her to his kiss. Her taut, sensitive breasts were tantalized by the mat of curling hair on his chest. When he rolled to his back, Brenna went along, sprawled half over him in a delicious tangle of limbs.

Kane's smile held a challenge. "Do you want me, babe?"

She took her time, settling comfortably atop him and bracing her hands on his shoulders, before she stopped to consider his question. Finally, with her eyes laughing down at him, she nodded. Just once.

"Good." There was a wealth of satisfaction in his voice. "Then come and get me."

"Whatever happened to chivalry?" Brenna mourned, sitting up straighter and easing her knees down on either side of his waist. "A man used to take a woman's hand and *lead* her."

"That's because he had all the power. Right now, you've got it, and you can have whatever you want." His warm palms settled on her thighs in a soft caress. "Whenever you want. However you want it."

Leaning forward so that the tips of her breasts brushed his chest, Brenna thought fleetingly that she didn't *want* power. She wanted love. Then she deliberately put the notion aside as Kane groaned and shifted beneath her. Tomorrow was for thinking, she told herself. Tonight was for...what? Pleasure? Yes, that, of course, but there was much, much more, she decided vaguely. A growing sense of certainty was telling her that without tonight, there was no chance at all for a tomorrow.

She stared down at Kane, the laughter suddenly gone as she absorbed the intensity beneath his humor. Without moving a muscle, he was drawing her in, tempting her, luring her closer. And even in the dim light of that small lamp across the room, she could see the vulnerability in his eyes. He allowed her to see it. No, she decided, he *wanted* her to see it. He was challenging her with the knowledge that he wasn't afraid to put himself in her hands—to trust her.

Brenna closed her eyes and bent her head. She felt his warm breath on her cheek but before their lips touched, she heard his whispered words.

"I love you, babe."

The taut silence in the room was broken by her sigh. She would know later that it was the exact moment of both victory and surrender. For both of them.

With a swift, shallow breath, she brushed her mouth against his, feeling the prickly darts of pleasure shimmering through her body. Kane moved his hands to her hips in a gliding caress.

They touched, shivered, moaned with gathering sensual tension, moving, arching against each other. Then Kane's hands tightened, lifting and guiding her home. She took his love and gave him her own. And when their breathing slowed down, Brenna heard her own husky whisper.

The words brushed over him in a soft litany. "...love you, love you...love you."

Sometime before dawn, in his massive bed with her fingers laced in his thick hair, Brenna arched against him. Half asleep, in the midst of a delightful dream, she felt his lips tugging gently at the tip of her breast. Murmuring in drowsy contentment at the gathering tension in her body, she was soothed by his whisper.

"It's all right, babe."

"Hmm."

His teeth closed delicately around her nipple for one melting second. "Where do you want to live when we're married?"

Brenna opened one eye and stared down at his dark head. Tightening her fingers so he wouldn't move, she said, "You're pushing, Matthews."

She could feel his smile.

"I know. I've got to get you while you're in a weakened state. Where?"

Brenna grinned. He *was* pushing, but this time it didn't matter. Because, finally, she was free of the past. She wasn't her mother—it was as simple as that. She was too strong to be a reflection of anyone. "I want to live here," she decided.

"Good." Kane moved his lips against her breast then propped himself up on his bent elbow. He tilted her face and dropped a small kiss on her love-swollen mouth before he turned onto his back and tucked her in the curve of his arm. "You've worn me out, woman. Let's get some sleep."

Kane opened the door and took the packages out of Brenna's hands. She let him keep the big, flat, hot box but took back the larger, square one.

"I brought the pizza, do you have the tape?" Ignoring his curious glance at the large carton, she leaned forward and kissed him.

It was Monday evening. Brenna had been in a seminar all day and Kane had jousted with Walton Kramer on TV.

"How did it go?" she asked nervously, nudging him toward the steps. "Did you do everything we practiced yesterday? Tell me everything about it. Every word. Were you nervous. *I* was. God only knows what I told those people today. Did he try to pull anything? Was he as devious as he usually is? Well?" They were at the top of the stairs and she didn't stop until she reached the couch by the television. "*Say* something."

Kane grinned and placed the pizza on the coffee table. Then he took the other, surprisingly light box out of Brenna's arms and put it on the floor. "You haven't given me a chance," he complained mildly, taking her into his arms. "I missed you. I haven't had a kiss since six-thirty this morning."

For the next few minutes, he remedied the situation with Brenna's enthusiastic cooperation.

"Mmm, very nice," she said breathlessly. "More later, please. But I can't wait another minute to see the tape. You got it all, didn't you."

Kane chuckled. "Every second."

"You look very pleased with yourself," she said, watching while he walked over to the VCR. She ran to the kitchen and grabbed a couple of plates and some napkins while he turned on the set. "It must have gone well. No! Don't tell me," she ordered when he turned and opened his mouth. "I want to *see* it."

He pointed to the couch. "Sit!"

She sat.

"And relax."

She couldn't.

"You're going to get indigestion, eating while you're this wound up. Should I put the pizza in the oven until the tape's over?"

"No." She opened the box and put a gigantic slice on each plate. "I always eat when I'm nervous. Turn it on."

Kane punched the button and sat down beside Brenna. He had never seen her so agitated. At least not over a business matter, he reflected with an inward smile. He wondered briefly if she agonized like this over all of her clients. He doubted it. This time, he let the smile show.

It didn't matter. Brenna was watching the television screen too intently to notice. She took a bite of pizza and chewed nervously while the credits flashed over shots of Kramer taken in dramatic scenes from past shows.

"Look at him," she muttered, while the host made his opening remarks.

"He's not a bad guy," Kane said comfortably. "It's a matter of showmanship. Done for the ratings."

"Yeah." She crunched her teeth into the crusty dough. "Ah. You look good. Not nervous." One part of her mind critiqued the action. Kane's voice was clear and decisive. He spoke in crisp, short sentences. He didn't use acronyms or buzz words that might be unfamiliar to the viewers. When asked to explain about the "virus" that infected programs, *she* even understood his explanation.

"Watch out!" she warned, watching Kramer's practiced smile. "He's working up to something." The camera cut to Kane's face and after one quick glance, she took a deep breath and relaxed a smidgen. "You're enjoying this," she decided.

Kane chuckled. "Wasn't that the idea?"

"The bastard! Listen to what he's saying!"

Kramer's mellifluous voice oozed out through the speaker. "You've garnered a generous share of government dollars in contracts over the past three years. Many more than your closest competitors. Some of them are wondering how you do it so consistently. Do you have any comment?"

Brenna exploded. "He's all but saying you're involved in bribes or some other kind of corruption."

Kane put his hand on her arm.

At the same time she heard the steel in his voice as, looking directly at the gray-haired moderator, he asked, "Are you saying that any of them implied I was less than ethical in my dealings with the government?"

Walton Kramer blinked at the direct attack and back-pedaled as fast as he could. The essence of his retraction was that perhaps he had phrased the question badly. Of course, there was no such implication.

The smile Kane directed at the flustered man was nothing less than brilliant. "I thought not," he told him in a velvety voice. "My comment, then, is that I get so many government contracts because I meet and exceed their requirements, with a zero defect record." Brenna recognized the renegade in the next statement. "Any man who knows what he's doing and is willing to work his butt off can do the same thing."

"Wahoo!" Brenna leaned over and kissed him on the cheek. "You've got him running." After that, there wasn't much doubt about who was in charge of the interview.

At one point, Kramer reeled off a convoluted question designed to draw Kane into a mire of complicated explanations. He ended by asking, "How would you handle this?"

Kane grinned and said, "I wouldn't touch it with a ten-foot pole." Then he waited amiably while Kramer's confident smile slipped and the older man scrambled through his notes for the next question.

Kramer's last effort was to drop a time-limit bomb. He commented that one of the early software firms, now defunct, was suing some existing companies—including Kane's—for using its early technology to produce the current software. They had ten seconds left. Would Kane state his position?

Kane shook his head with genuine regret. "It's impossible to do so in ten seconds. If you'll invite me back, I'll be delighted to discuss it at length."

The camera panned quickly over Kramer's expression of frustration and settled on Kane's amiable smile.

Brenna placed her empty plate on the table and threw herself into Kane's arms, pressing against him when he pulled her across his thighs. "Revenge is sweet," she crowed. "You got back at him for all the rotten things he's done." Then she sighed deeply.

"What?"

"Oh, nothing. It's silly."

"What?" He tightened his arms.

"I just wish..."

"What?"

She sighed again and spoiled it with a gurgle of laughter. "That you had worn a sign around your neck that said, 'Excellent presentation due in part to Brenna MacKay, A Touch of Class.' It would have been wonderful publicity."

Leaning back against his shoulder, she relaxed for the first time that day. Tapping a slim finger against his chin, she waited until he looked down at her. "You done good," she assured him.

Before he could say a word, she sat up and slid off his lap. "I almost forgot," she exclaimed. "I got you something."

She handed him the large, square box and sat back down on the couch, facing him while he opened it.

He looked at her. "For me?"

She smiled, nodding. Like most men, Kane was slightly awkward when on the receiving end of a gift.

"What's the occasion?" He touched the bright blue bow, but made no move to open it.

How typical, she thought. This man of hers even had to analyze the reason behind a gift. This man of hers who was so many men in one. He was cool and very hot, vulnerable and tough, funny and wise, pushy and protective. And he was hers. Forever.

"Occasion?" she repeated. "Let's just say that I finally made up my mind."

He slanted another glance at her, then tore off the paper. Impatiently he snapped the tape and pulled out wads of tissue paper. He looked down and stopped, taking a deep, ragged breath. Slowly he reached into the box and lifted out a snowy white Stetson.

His eyes met hers. "The good guy?"

Brenna nodded, holding his gaze. At the same time, she reached out and dumped the box on the floor. "He always wears white," she reminded him.

While he put the hat on his head and tugged at the brim, she moved back onto his lap and began to unbutton his shirt. She could feel the pounding of his heart as she worked her way from one button to the next.

Tilting her face up for his kiss, she murmured against his lips, "And he always gets his woman."

*   *   *   *   *

Silhouette Special Edition

presents

★ LOVE AND GLORY ★

from
Lindsay McKenna

Introducing a gripping new series celebrating our men—and women—in uniform. Meet the Trayherns, a military family as proud and colorful as the American flag, a family fighting the shadow of dishonor, a family determined to triumph—with **LOVE AND GLORY!**

June: A QUESTION OF HONOR (SE #529) leads the fast-paced excitement. When Coast Guard officer Noah Trayhern offers Kit Anderson a safe house, he unwittingly endangers his own guarded emotions.

July: NO SURRENDER (SE #535) Navy pilot Alyssa Trayhern's assignment with arrogant jet jockey Clay Cantrell threatens her career—and her heart—with a crash landing!

August: RETURN OF A HERO (SE #541) Strike up the band to welcome home a man whose top-secret reappearance will make headline news . . . with a delicate, daring woman by his side.

Three courageous siblings—
three consecutive months of

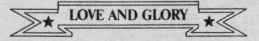

★ LOVE AND GLORY ★

Premiering in **June**, only in
Silhouette Special Edition.

LG-1

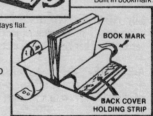